Almost Murder

RODERIC JEFFRIES

Almost Murder

An Inspector Alvarez Novel

St. Martin's Press
New York

Library of Congress Cataloging in Publication Data

Ashford, Jeffrey, 1926-
  Almost murder.

   I. Title.
PR6060.E43A74   1986   823'.914   86-1857
ISBN 0-312-02137-2

First published in Great Britain by William Collins Sons & Co. Ltd.

First U.S. Edition

10 9 8 7 6 5 4 3 2 1

CHAPTER 1

Æons ago, the river had flowed so forcefully that it had carved out the softer rock to form a bottle-shaped mouth; then the climate had changed and its strength had been diminished until, in the form of a torrente, it appeared only after heavy rain in the mountains. The sea invaded the inlet to form a natural harbour and this was popular with inshore fishing-boats because it was protected from everything but a heavy south-easter.

When the foreigners invaded the island, they demanded moorings for their pleasure craft and before long the fishing-boats, by now greatly reduced in numbers, were ordered to the far end of the inlet where the water was shallow and underwater rocks called for more expert navigation than most of the foreigners could command, especially after a generous lunch. As the fishermen discovered, in modern society there was never any doubt about the relative importance of the work of those who provided the essentials of life.

The *Aphrodite* lay at the penultimate berth on the harbour arm which formed the outer breakwater and gave protection against the occasional south-easter. She was a 26-metre Benetti with twin Caterpillar engines; her hull was painted a light blue and her upperworks white. Registered in Southampton, she flew the flag of the Amington Yacht Club, a griffon on the red ensign.

Aft of the saloon was open deck, and chairs and a table had been set out on the holystoned teak deck. Todd looked at his slim gold Baume and Mercier. 'Where the hell's the man got to?'

Kendall chuckled. 'He's probably got a puncture and is standing around waiting for someone to show him what to do.'

'I said to be here at eleven, sharp.'

'We're not all split-second men like you, Deiny.'

'I wish you'd remember not to call me that.'

'Deiniol seems such a mouthful. The Welsh complicate everything, including the names of their railway stations. What's that one with fifty-eight letters?'

'I've no idea.'

'I'm sure that admission would lose you votes in the hills.'

Todd looked as if he were about to comment sharply, but then shrugged his shoulders. He was an immediately recognizable man, thanks mainly to television; women invariably referred to him as handsome, men, perhaps from jealousy, often said that he was far too smooth. Only when he forgot to control his expression was there more than a hint of the steel which lay beneath the charm. He turned and faced for'd. 'Félix,' he shouted.

A moment later, Rullán walked through the saloon. 'We go?' he asked, his English heavily accented, but comprehensible.

'Not yet, Señor Leach isn't here. But we'll have a drink. Bring a couple of glasses and one of the bottles of champagne in the refrigerator; not one from the wine rack.'

Rullán returned the way he had come.

'Ten to one,' said Todd, 'he'll bring the wrong bottle.'

'If there's a way of doing something wrong, the locals will find it, even if that means working at the problem. As I always tell my clients, forget the way things are done back home because they won't be done like that out here.' Kendall smiled broadly. A man who had had little cause to like him had once compared him to a butter-ball into which it would be a pleasure to run a hot knife. He'd smiled even when he'd come as close as 200,000 pesetas to being locked up in a Spanish jail.

Rullán returned with two tulip-shaped glasses and a bottle of Codorníu *brut* on a silver salver. He set the salver on the table, picked up the bottle, stripped off the foil and wire, skilfully eased out the cork. He poured a little of the champagne into Todd's glass. Todd waved his hand to show he couldn't be bothered with tasting and Rullán filled Kendall's glass and then his.

'Put the bottle back in the fridge,' said Todd, 'and make certain you put the cap on—do you know which cap I mean?'

'Yes, señor.'

'Putting a spoon in the neck is just as good at keeping the bubbles in,' said Kendall.

'I've heard that,' replied Todd, in tones of complete disbelief.

'I've come to the conclusion that there's nothing like a glass of bubbly before midday to make one feel delightfully guilty . . . It's a funny thing, but Kay doesn't like it; she'd much rather have orange juice.' He chuckled. 'As some sage once remarked, women just aren't made the same. Which at times is just as well, isn't it?'

Todd ignored the fatuous comment. He looked at his watch again.

'You know something, Deiny . . . Sorry, Deiniol. Anyone can tell you don't live here. You worry about the time.'

'I made it perfectly clear I wanted to set sail by a quarter past eleven.'

'Relax. This is Spain, where the only thing which starts on time is the bullfight. What if Cyril is a few minutes late?'

'Nearly an hour.'

'All right, nearly an hour. Out here, you're early until you're at least half an hour late. Count your blessings, as my maternal aunt used to say whenever her husband tried to borrow money from her. Look at our blessings. The sun's shining, we're drinking some very acceptable bubbly, and in the next boat there's a blonde with as neat a superstructure as I've seen on any vassal. Not, of course, that you'd be interested in anything so pedestrian.'

Todd looked sharply at Kendall, but the broad grin, which

creased his round, plump face, concealed any emotion other than a crude, apparently thoughtless good humour.

'But talking about the ladies, God bless 'em, Kay said to ask you if you'll come over for dinner one evening. And, of course, any friend you like to bring. Nothing grand, I'm afraid. But if it would amuse you to slum for one night?' Once again, it was impossible accurately to judge whether there was mockery behind his words.

'I'm afraid I'm busy right up until I return home.'

'Kay'll be very disappointed. Never let on I told you, but we were lent a tape the other night and one of the programmes had you castigating the latest example of government stupidity. She said you made her feel all young and uncertain again. Uncertain about what? I asked.' He laughed loudly.

Rullán came aft, his rope-soled shoes creating a gentle slapping sound. 'We no go?'

'We go when I say,' replied Todd shortly.

'Is nearly twelve hours . . .'

'I know damn well what the time is.'

'Yes, señor.' Rullán, his wrinkled, tanned face expressing no particular resentment, left.

Kendall, who sat facing the quayside, suddenly said; 'Here at long last comes our intrepid yachtsman. Now there's tone for you! Makes us look like a couple of bargees.'

Todd turned to stare at the oncoming man. 'Bloody fool,' he said contemptuously.

Leach was wearing a peaked cap, white yachting jacket bright with brass buttons, and white tailored ducks. He could have stepped out of a 1910 photograph of Cowes.

He climbed the short gangway with very great care, holding tightly on to the rope. His thin, oval face was flushed and sweat was trickling down his cheeks. 'I do hope . . .'

'You're an hour late,' said Todd, brusquely interrupting his apologies.

'The trouble was, some people dropped in just as I was

getting ready to leave and they weren't in a hurry to go.'

'You didn't think of telling them to get a move on?' Todd drained his glass, set it on the table.

'But you can't say that sort of thing, can you?'

Todd didn't bother to answer.

'You see, I didn't want to upset them.'

'Hoping that you wouldn't upset us even more if you were late?' asked Kendall, with malicious amusement.

Leach flushed. He looked at Todd, then away; he never looked directly at anyone for long.

'Since you have finally condescended to arrive,' said Todd, 'perhaps we can at last sail.'

'Hoist the main topgallant staysail,' exclaimed Kendall.

Todd stood and went for'd through the saloon on his way to the wheelhouse. They heard him calling for Rullán.

'He sounds . . . a bit annoyed?' said Leach.

'You know our Deiny. If he says such and such is to happen, he's personally affronted if it doesn't.'

'But it really was terribly difficult for me.'

'Naturally.'

'This couple, the Pritchards . . . Well, they've always been a bit distant before. So when they turned up, I simply had to ask them in for a drink. I mean, if I hadn't, they might have thought . . .' He tailed off into an uncomfortable silence.

'Cyril, old man, let me give you a piece of priceless advice. And don't look so worried, I'm not going to charge for it.' Kendall laughed heartily. 'Stop worrying about what other people think. Most of 'em out here can't.'

'But I . . . Well, I . . .'

'And you know the best way of dealing with people who act like there's a bad smell under their noses? Show 'em you don't care and at the same time give 'em something to chew on. You ought to have told 'em you couldn't ask 'em in because you had to rush off for a day on the briny with the Great Deiniol Todd. Or were you scared of sounding as if you were boasting? Remember, success in this world never favours the discreet. D'you imagine I sell a house by admitting the truth—that it was built by a one-armed waiter in his time off, that it suffers so badly from rising damp that there's no need for a glass bowl for the goldfish, and that if it's standing in ten years' time it'll be a miracle. Not bloody likely! The builder won a gold medal at an exhibition, the interior is so dry even Spanish cornflakes become crisp, and when the Pyramids are a heap of rubble it'll still be there.'

Rullán came aft and as he drew level with the table, they felt the deck vibrate as first one and then the other engine was started.

'Here,' said Kendall in his easy, ungrammatical Spanish, 'we've a tragedy in the making, Félix; Señor Leach hasn't anything to drink. So bring us that bottle from the fridge, will you?'

'Señor, I have to cast off . . .'

'A couple more minutes won't grow any extra barnacles.'

Leach said nervously: 'Are you asking him to bring me a drink? D'you think you ought to? I mean, Deiniol hasn't actually offered me one yet.'

'Only because he lacks manners.' Kendall spoke to Rullán again. 'And will you bring another glass with the bottle.'

Rullán turned and went back into the saloon.

Kendall looked across the table. 'You won't mind if I give you a bit more free advice, will you? Never worry about other people until you're satisfied that numero uno is doing all right.'

'But . . .'

'No buts if you want to survive in this shark-infested world.'

'There was a call from the bridge. 'Let go aft.'

Leach said: 'Félix isn't there. D'you think we ought to do something?'

'D'you know which rope does what?'

'Not really.'

'Then let someone else sort things out.'

There was another, much more impatient call from the bridge.

'Now he's getting angry because the great panjandrum isn't being instantly obeyed,' said Kendall. 'The theory is that no one can hide his true character from the camera. Complete cods'. See Deiny on the box and you'd really think he was all open-hearted generosity; you'd never guess that in fact he's one of the most selfish men alive and so conceited that his best friend is a mirror.'

'I wouldn't say that . . .'

'I know you wouldn't; that's your big problem.'

Rullán hurried out, put a glass and the bottle of champagne on the table, continued aft. He let got of the port stern line and hauled it in, let go of the starboard line and as soon as it was clear of the water shouted: 'All OK aft.'

Kendall filled the two glasses. 'So long as the sea's glass-calm and there's bubbly in my glass, I'm quite ready to be a jolly jack tar.'

'I often used to dream about owning a boat. Not as big as this one, of course.'

'Why the "of course"?'

As Rullán passed them, going for'd, Leach looked blankly at Kendall.

'For God's sake, if you're going to dream, dream QE Two size.'

The *Aphrodite* slowly moved out of her berth, then turned to port to head for the harbour entrance. The sky was cloudless, the sun fierce, and there would be no relief from the burning heat until she was making a headwind. Kendall drank, took a handkerchief from the pocket of his trousers and mopped the sweat from his forehead and neck. He refilled his glass. He thoroughly enjoyed other peoples' champagne.

The coast lay five miles to the north, the image of the tall, bleak cliffs distorted by the heat haze so that they appeared to be shimmering. The sea was calm, but there was a southerly swell which kept the boat moving rhythmically as she sailed at slow speed, under the control of the automatic pilot. Only one other craft was in sight, a fishing-boat out on the starboard quarter, partially hull down.

When issuing the invitation, Todd had referred to a snack meal, but he was incapable of doing anything simply. They'd started with very generous portions of smoked salmon, continued with quail cooked in the Mallorquin style with serrano ham, and were finishing with plums in brandy and/or cheese and biscuits. They'd drunk two bottles of Imperial, one white and one red, and a second red one had just been opened.

Rullán offered Kendall the shaped board on which were half a dozen different cheeses. Kendall picked up the forked-tip knife. 'This looks like the monarch of them all, Roquefort.'

'It's Austrian blue,' corrected Todd.

'Of course. How stupid of me. The Roquefort's kept for your important guests.'

Todd was visibly annoyed by this gratuitous rudeness. 'Hasn't it ever occurred to you . . .' He stopped, drained his glass.

'Hasn't it ever occurred to me to what?'

'Nothing.'

'Come on, tell the truth and shame the devil.'

'I've never rated you that highly.'

'Now is that a compliment? Or is it not? Big white chief speak with forked tongue.'

Rullán, who'd been holding the cheeseboard in front of Kendall all this time, put it down on the table. 'I go see OK.' He went for'd into the saloon and then up the short companionway.

'He seems to be very conscientious,' said Leach.

Normally, so vapid a comment would have drawn a smile from Kendall and have been ignored by Todd. But even though they had drunk heavily, they could still appreciate the need to stay on neutral ground if they were to avoid an open row.

'He is,' said Todd shortly.

'I don't agree with what other people say.'

'As any politician will tell you, a very wise precaution.' Kendall cut himself a very generous slice of Brie.

'I've always found the Mallorquins completely reliable,' went on Leach.

Kendall refilled his glass. 'I wonder if one refers to that as a miracle or a delusion?'

'They're no worse than anyone else.'

'Hardly much of a standard.'

'If they go on and on about money, it's our fault.'

'Speak for yourself.'

'I'm speaking for all the foreigners. It's we who've come here and upset all their values. It's no wonder they dislike us.' In his excitement, Leach had begun to wave his hands around; he knocked a knife off the table with such force that it went spinning across the deck and out through the doorway. Red-faced, mumbling apologies, he stood and, his movements clumsy both because of the wine and the motion of the boat, he left the table and walked aft.

'You feel disliked?' shouted Kendall ironically. 'I find that very hard to believe!'

Leach reached the outside deck, squinted heavily in the burning sunlight as he looked for the knife. He saw it had come to rest to his right. He stepped across and bent down to pick it up. At that moment, the boat rolled heavily and out of rhythm and he was caught off balance and he fell to the deck in a tangle of arms and legs. And it was because he was now fortuitously protected by the bulkhead, on the far side of which was a settee which was also a locker containing kapok lifejackets, that he was not blasted into death as were the other two, by the explosion which tore their world apart.

CHAPTER 2

A fly landed on the desk. Alvarez watched it stroll towards the pile of letters which had arrived by the morning's post and were, as yet, unopened. Life, he decided, had been over-generous to flies. Nothing to do and all day in which to do it. A far cry from his own tension-ridden life in which he was lucky if he had a single minute that he could call his own. The fly climbed up the side of the first, and thickest, envelope. That, he was certain, contained a further, and probably more peremptory, request for five witness statements, a request originally made some weeks before. Why did he have to be burdened with other people's problems when he had so many of his own?

The fly flew off towards the unshuttered, open window and when it passed through and became lost to sight he followed it in his mind's eye, his envy increasing. Complete freedom, no one to consider but itself . . . The sun was not yet shining into the room, but the day was hot and he was tired. His eyelids slid shut. He began to drift into space as freely as the fly . . .

The telephone rang. It went on ringing. He opened his eyes. Couldn't the damn fool at the other end realize there was no one in the office? he wondered resentfully. Evidently the damn fool couldn't. He finally leaned over and picked up the reciever.

'I have a call for you from Superior Chief Salas,' said Salas's secretary in her plum-laden voice.

It was obviously going to be one of those days, he thought with added gloom.

As ever, Salas did not bother with any social greetings, but then he came from Madrid. 'Have you heard about the deaths of the two Englishmen off Cala Vescari on the third?'

'When exactly was that, señor?'

'Are you saying you don't even know the date?'

He looked across at the calendar on the far wall, but that was of little immediate help since he had not yet torn off the sheet for May.

'Two days ago, three Englishmen went out in a boat with a Mallorquin crew member. When at sea, there was an explosion; two of the Englishmen were killed, the third and the crewman were injured. One of the dead was a member of the British parliament which means that this is a very serious incident indeed.'

Alvarez did not agree—dead MPs tended to cause far less trouble then live ones—but he remained silent. Salas had little sense of humour and an exaggerated respect for the Establishment.

'Until yesterday, it had been assumed that the explosion was accidental; the boat carried bottled gas and this produces a well recorded hazard aboard boats. But yesterday I received a call from the English police which may put things in a very different light. Señor Todd, the MP, has been very closely connected with a campaign aimed at increasing the penalties for convicted terrorists. His work has received considerable international publicity and recently he's had several threatening communications from terrorist organizations. The last one received by post three weeks ago was from a group calling itself the Shining Sword of Allah.

'A Spanish speaking member of the anti-terrorist squad at New Scotland Yard told me that very little is known about this group beyond the probable facts that it is of Middle East origin, is largely funded by Libya, and its declared aim is to destabilize Western society. It is not thought to be a large organization, but its members are of a fanatical character. Señor Jennings also told me that they have recently carried out two bombings, one in France, one in Germany; in each case, the evidence suggested considerable expertise. He offered to send one of his most experienced officers to help us if we decided this explosion probably was the work of terrorists.'

'That'll be very helpful.'

Salas said coldly: 'I thanked Señor Jennings, but informed him that we are more than capable of conducting any investigation efficiently . . . The circumstances being as I've just described, I trust that even you will begin to appreciate that the work must be carried out with total competency.'

'Of course, señor. But I do think I ought to point out that if this was an act of terrorism, then the terrorists will surely have left the island by now and be beyond arrest. Of course, we'll have to establish whether it was, in fact, an act of terrorism, but if we do then there can't be any guarantee . . .'

'Alvarez, what in the devil are you babbling on about?'

'I'm trying to explain, señor, why my inquiries aren't likely to . . .'

'Your inquiries? Do you seriously think I'd ever dare leave you in charge of a case of this importance? I asked for Comisario Suau to be sent from the Peninsula and he is in Cala Vescari now. Since he speaks only a little English and has in the past not had many dealings with foreigners, I have decided—reluctantly—to assign you to help him. You will report to him immediately.'

Alvarez said hurriedly: 'Señor, in the past few weeks I've been snowed under with work which I can't afford to neglect . . .'

'But no doubt have succeeded in so doing. Immediately, is that clear?' Salas rang off.

Alvarez replaced the receiver and sighed. He thought for a moment, then dialled a friend.

'Have I heard of Comisario Suau!' said García. He laughed and his deep, booming laugh suggested he was large, fat, and dedicated to the pleasures of life.

'What's he like?'

'Meanest little bastard out. Why d'you want to know?'

'The superior chief's called him over to take charge of a case and I'm to work with him.'

'What a combination! Tell you what, if it's any consolation to know, I'll order some really nice flowers to put on your grave.'

A few minutes later, Alvarez rang off. What had he ever done to deserve so crushing a fate? He leaned over and opened the bottom right-hand drawer of the desk and brought out a bottle of brandy and a glass.

Cala Vescari lay on the south coast and the drive from Llueso took Alvarez across the central plain of the island, through towns which saw few foreigners and past countryside which varied from rich, irrigated fields to poor, rocky soil, parched from May to October and capable of growing little beyond almonds and one very light crop of grain. The town provided a sharp and unwelcome contrast with the countryside, whether rich or poor, and owed its present size solely to the tourist trade, a fact that became obvious as soon as the roadside became bordered by hoardings in English and German and the first of the new, boxy houses appeared just over the brow of the last rise.

Eventually, and after one totally wrong set of directions, Alvarez found the police station belonging to the Policía Armada y de Tráfico. He parked and went inside. The uniform sergeant on duty said with complete indifference that he'd never heard of Comisario Suau, but further inquiries established the fact that the Comisario had been given a room on the third floor. Alvarez climbed the steep flights of stairs, his pace becoming slower and slower because of shortage of breath and reluctance.

Suau was a small man with a neat, sharply featured face; his black hair was kept immaculate with haircream, he shaved twice a day so that he should never suffer a five o'clock shadow, and his tight moustache was the epitome of trimness. His fingers were long and shapely, almost musical, and he used them with quick, neat precision, whether adjusting the knot of his tie or signing his name with character and clarity. He spoke with clipped speed and never wasted words. He always dressed with careful formality and even in the present heat was wearing a lightweight suit.

When Alvarez entered the office, he had been reading some papers. He looked up and in only a few seconds he examined and judged. 'Yes, what d'you want?' he asked, impatient of the interruption.

'Señor, I am Inspector Alvarez, from Llueso.'

Suau showed considerable astonishment.

'Superior Chief Salas has directed me . . .'

Suau interrupted. 'To report here immediately. It is now just over two hours since he informed me you were coming, yet I understand that the journey from Llueso cannot possibly take more than three-quarters of an hour.'

'Before I left, I had various matters to arrange . . .'

'We may find it easier to work together if you understand from the beginning that I am uninterested in excuses.'

'But I couldn't just drop everything . . .'

'And kindly remember something else. I expect my staff at all times to dress respectably and not to appear before me looking like tramps.'

Tramp? thought Alvarez. Perhaps his shirt did have a small stain on the right breast—the arroz a la marinera the previous night had been delicious—his trousers were slightly crumpled, and now that he thought about it, he was fairly certain he'd forgotten to shave that morning, but tramp . . . ?

Suau squared up the papers on the desk, pushed back his chair, and stood. 'Since you are finally here, we'll go to the clinic to interview Señor Leach.'

'That means driving to Palma, señor.'

'Of course.'

'Then I suggest we eat first. By the time we get there, we'll find all the reasonable restaurants terribly crowded and . . .'

'I have no intention of wasting time eating in a restaurant. If the opportunity arises, we'll have a sandwich.'

Alvarez's cup of misery overflowed.

The clinic was situated on rising land on the outskirts of Palma; from it there were views both of the mountains to the north and the bay to the south. Leach was in a room on the second floor. Still shocked and frightened, he was constantly fiddling with the sheet which was his only covering as he lay on the bed. Through Alvarez, Suau introduced himself and formally expressed the hope that Leach would soon be better. Then he moved the only chair closer to the bed and sat, leaving Alvarez to settle on the settee which could be converted into a bed when, as was normal, a relative accompanied the patient.

'Señor Leach, you live in Palma?'

'I've a flat. On the Paseo Marítimo.' Leach spoke in jerky, abrupt sentences, his voice strained.

'How long have you lived there?'

'Between three and four years. I don't know exactly.'

'You possess a residencia?'

'Yes.'

'May I see it, please?'

'I haven't got it. I keep it at home . . .'

Suau's tight lips tightened. The law said that an identity card or residencia should be carried at all times. There was no exception for those in hospital.

'When did you first know you were going on the boat trip?'

'Deiniol rang up and suggested it; I suppose that was Friday or Saturday.'

'Are you married?'

'Yes, but . . . but my wife lives in England.'

'Do you employ anyone to do the housework?'

'I . . . yes.' He suffered sharp embarrassment.

'Did you tell her you were going on this trip?'

'I . . . I can't remember.'

'Did you mention it to any of your friends?'

'I can't . . . I'm sorry, I don't seem to be able to think clearly.'

'Please try harder.'

'It's not easy, not after being blown up,' he said, with weak petulance. When Suau showed no reaction to his words, he struggled to collect his thoughts. 'I do seem to remember telling Ken.'

'Who is he?'

'Ken Street. He and Madge live in Magalluf. He was in the army, but they're still nice . . . What I mean is, retired army officers can be very . . . and their wives are even worse. But Madge isn't like that at all.'

'Can you say when you told them?'

'It must have been when I had drinks with them. On Sunday.'

'Did you tell anyone else?'

'I'm pretty certain I didn't, no.'

'So as far as you know at the moment, only your friends, the Streets, and perhaps your maid, were aware that you were going to be on the boat on Tuesday?'

'That's right.'

'Will you decribe what happened on Tusday.'

His fingers plucked much more quickly at the sheet.

'I'm sorry if it brings back very unpleasant memories, señor, but we have to know exactly what happened.'

He swallowed heavily several times, reached up with his right hand and gently touched a slight swelling on the side of his jaw.

'When did you leave your flat?'

'I was late because the Pritchards called unexpectedly.'

'They are friends of yours?'

'That's right. Except I'd call them more acquaintances, if you know what I mean.'

'Did you tell them where you were going?'

'I might have done.'

'But they did not know beforehand?'

'No.'

'Then what was the time when you left?'

'I suppose it was something like half past eleven.'

'Did you drive straight to Cala Vescari?'

'I knew I was going to be very late and Deiniol always gets so annoyed if one's not dead on time . . .' He stopped abruptly as he realized that in the circumstances this was an infelicitous phrase to have used.

'Where did you park your car?'

'On the harbour arm. There was just room.'

'Were there many people around at that time?'

'There did seem to be, yes.'

'Did you board right away?'

'Yes. I was in such a hurry.'

'And did the boat sail soon afterwards?'

'Immediately. Deiniol was in quite a state because I was late. But as I tried to explain . . .' He became silent.

'Did you look back at the quayside at all as you sailed?'

'I don't really remember but I suppose I must have done. After all, Arthur and I were sitting out on the deck.'

'Where was Señor Todd?'

'He was at the wheel.'

'And Rullán?'

'Félix? He was busy with ropes and fenders.'

'Were you conscious of any smell of gas?'

'No, not at all.'

'Do you think you would have noticed it if there had been such a smell?'

'I'm sure I would; I've a very keen nose.'

'Did Señor Todd ever mention a gas leak?'

'Never.'

'Did he suggest there was any other sort of trouble?'

'Only me not arriving on time.'

'Did you notice anything in the boat which struck you as

unusual or out of place; something like a package or a suitcase?'

'No, I didn't.'

'What were you doing immediately before the explosion?'

It was some time before Leach answered and when he did his voice was so low that Alvarez had difficulty in understanding him; his expression had become one of fear remembered. 'We were having lunch. Félix was trying to serve Arthur with cheese, but Arthur was so busy talking that in the end he put the board down and went up to the bridge to make certain everything was all right. After he'd gone, we had a bit of a discussion and I got . . . Well, I got a bit excited and knocked a knife off the table and it went shooting out on deck. So I went out to pick it up. Then the boat rolled and sent me flying and as I hit the deck, there was the explosion.'

'Can you describe the explosion?'

'Not really . . . I mean, except it seemed to be all light and blast and funnily not much noise.'

'What happened next?'

'I found myself in the sea. The boat was in two and sinking and it hurt more and more to move and anyway I've always been a bit of a poor swimmer . . . It was certain I was going to drown . . .'

Suau's expression became faintly contemptuous. He believed that a man should show death a courageous face. Since he'd never been called upon to do so, his belief was strong.

Sweat had formed on Leach's forehead. 'I shouted and shouted for help. I was certain I was the only person alive . . .' He paused, then said in the tones of a confession: 'I even wished I'd gone with the others and not been left to die slowly . . .'

Suau was not the man to try to ease the pain of the memory. 'That's all we need to know for the moment,' he said to Alvarez in Spanish.

Alvarez, ignoring him, said to Leach: 'What kind of a person was Señor Todd?'

'I . . . I don't understand,' mumbled Leach, still caught up in the horror of his near-drowning.

'Were you very friendly with him?'

'I can't really say that. I mean, his style of life was so different. He knew all the important people.'

Suau said impatiently: 'What are you saying to him?'

'I was asking what kind of a man Señor Todd was,' Alvarez replied.

'Why?'

'I've always thought it a good idea to build up a picture of peoples' characters . . .'

'One of the basic requirements of a good detective is to be able to distinguish between what is relevant and what is not. It hasn't occurred to you that if this was an act of terrorism, it is irrelevant whether Señor Todd was a saint or a sinner?'

'It's just . . . Well, one never knows.'

'For some people, that is exactly so.' Suau stood. The interview was over.

CHAPTER 3

The road from Palma to Cala Vescari had been improved some years before and now it by-passed all but one of the towns which lay along its route. Much of the countryside was open and fields were considerably larger than those on other parts of the island, but since there was little water for irrigation, these were not intensively cultivated; it was no-ticeable that there were few citrus, almond, and algarroba trees, but a number of what had once been prickly pear cactus plantations.

Suau drove with a total disregard for other users of the road and Alvarez—himself not the most careful of drivers —spent much of the journey with his eyes closed, praying to St Christopher. A silence which had lasted over five

kilometres was broken when Suau said: 'When we reach
Cala Vescari, you are to speak to the harbourmaster to find
whether any wreckage has been recovered; if it has, see it's
sent right away to the laboratory. Question the staff of the
café near the berth and the staff of the Club Nautico. Find out
if any of them noticed someone on Tuesday who was
obviously keeping watch on the boat.'

'I don't suppose there's much chance of that. At this time
of the season they'll have been working flat out and there'll
have been so many people wandering around . . .'

'Inspector, a case is not solved by enumerating all the
difficulties.'

'No, of course not, all I was . . .'

'It is solved by working with intelligent enthusiasm.'

'All I was trying to point out . . .' He stopped abruptly as
Suau crossed a solid line to overtake a lorry on a slight bend
and they came face to face with an oncoming van. He shut his
eyes and wondered whether Dolores, Jaime, Juan, and
Isabel, would put flowers on his grave every All Saints Day.
There was an angry blast of horn and the car lurched to the
right, but no horrifying impact.

'You've obviously failed to appreciate the significance of
the times involved.'

Alvarez opened his eyes. 'What . . . what did you say?'

'Do you find it very difficult to concentrate?'

'Not usually . . . But I thought we were going to hit that
van.'

'So we would have done, but for my skill . . . I said, you
have not grasped the significance of the times involved.'

'No, señor.'

'The *Aphrodite* was due to sail at eleven; it did not, in fact,
sail until after twelve. If there was a bomb aboard, this must
have been activated by either a timing mechanism or remote
control; we can ignore a third method, a trembler device,
because even when a boat is tied up it's always likely to be on
the move up and down. In either of the first two cases, it is

very probable that at least one of the terrorists will have been in the vicinity to watch the boat sail and when it failed to do so at the pre-arranged time, he will have become worried and uncertain. If the fuse was time-controlled, it might well activate when the boat was still tied up and their plan must have been to have the boat sink out at sea; if remote-controlled, delay as such was not potentially disastrous, but there would be the possibility that the delay was caused by their plan having been uncovered. A nervous, worried man is one who draws attention to himself even if the person whose attention is drawn is uncertain why this should be. That is why I have told you to question the staff; that is why, contrary to your pessimistic expectations, there is a reasonable chance one of them will have particularly noticed someone.'

'I suppose so . . . Only if it was a time-bomb, would the bomber have hung around and risked being blown up with the boat?'

'Perhaps,' said Suau, with silky sarcasm, 'you are forgetting that the bomb did not explode until approximately a quarter to two? There would have been no danger to him until shortly before that time.'

They drove down the gently sloping road into Cala Vescari and parked in front of the police station, in the shade of some pines. Alvarez opened his door.

'After you have questioned the staff at the café and Club Nautico, question Rullán.'

'It'll be pretty late by then and I do have to drive to Llueso . . .'

Suau might not have heard him. 'I managed to have a brief word with Rullán yesterday, but he's a man of mean intelligence and it was difficult to get any sense out of him.' He paused, just long enough for the inference to be clear when he said: 'Perhaps you will find it easier to communicate with him than I did.'

*

Alvarez walked along the harbour arm, came to a halt in front of a large motor-cruiser. What ever sized income did one need in order to be able to run a boat like that? Yet if he had such money, he'd never be such a fool as to spend it on a boat, he'd buy hectares of rich, irrigated land and he'd farm them. Land was forever . . .

The harbourmaster's office was half way along the arm and was part of a one-storey building which was also used to house some of the gear of the fishermen who still worked from the harbour. It consisted of one small room which was filled with table, chart table, filing cabinets, and glass-fronted bookcase: somewhat fortunately, the harbourmaster was a small man who did not need very much space. In answer to Alvarez's question, he waved his right hand in the direction of the single window, which faced the sea. 'I've chartered a fishing-boat and they're out there now, searching.'

'So you wouldn't know if they've found anything yet?'

'That's right.' He tugged at a quiff of grey, wiry hair.

'D'you think they will find anything?'

'How can I tell?' he answered impatiently.

'Experience might help.'

'D'you think the sea works by rules?'

Alvarez smiled briefly. 'I wouldn't know how it works.'

The harbourmaster made a sound of derision. 'That's obvious enough.'

'But since the boat did blow up, there'll have been lots of bits and pieces; some of them will surely still be floating around?'

'Are you telling or asking? I've known boats go down and you could almost rebuild 'em from the wreckage; I've known 'em go down and leave nothing.'

'When d'you expect the search boat back?'

'When they've finished.'

'They're making a really good search?'

'Listen, d'you reckon to do the job better?'

'Of course not.'

'Then leave 'em to get on with it.'

'My boss is a nut case who wants everything checked up ten times.'

'Then tell him it's Vicente Carbonell's boat and he knows the waters and the currents round here better than your boss knows himself. And on top of that, it was Vicente who saw the *Aphrodite* explode, so he knows to a metre where it happened.'

'That sounds good.'

'You try and do better.' The harbourmaster's manner became slightly less aggressive. 'Vicente was glad of the job because he's had a couple of poor days; the fishing's not what it was.'

'What is?'

'I don't know what is, I only know what isn't.'

'I've heard before that the Mediterranean's over-fished.'

'It may be, but the real trouble is, the youngsters of today don't like work and fishing's work, if anything is.'

'Who's going to work his guts out when there are tourists to be plucked?'

'It's all wrong,' replied the harbourmaster, with the satisfaction of a man who owned three flats which were let to tourists throughout the season and on which he paid not a peseta's tax.

Alvarez left and stepped out into the sun-drenched heat outside. Nearly at the end of the arm was an empty berth and he made his way to it through the strolling holidaymakers. The *Aphrodite* had sailed from here. Had there on Tuesday morning been a man, standing near where he was now standing, who had experienced an ever-growing tension because there was a bomb aboard the *Aphrodite*, timed to go off just before two o'clock, and the minutes were ticking away and the boat was still tied up? If there had been, surely he wouldn't have stood still for any length of time, but would have moved with the ever-changing crowd? So would anyone have noticed him, even if he had been under such tension?

Alvarez turned to look back at the café and the Club Nautico. A large number of tables were set outside both places, but even so, almost every table was occupied and the waiters were having to work very hard; it seemed unreasonable to expect any of them to have noticed a man who was taking what steps he could not to be noticed. Alvarez sighed. Suau had ordered him to make inquiries, so make them he must.

He walked down the arm to the café and threaded his way between tables to one that was empty. Gratefully, he slumped down in the shade of the sun umbrella. A waiter, in white shirt damp from sweat and black trousers, hurried up to the table. 'What'll it be, then?' he asked in Mallorquin, immediately identifying Alvarez as no tourist.

'A coñac, with plenty of ice. And when you've brought it, a bit of a talk.'

'Are you crazy? A talk, with me rushed off my feet?'

'Inspector Alvarez, Cuerpo General de Policía.'

The waiter's expression changed. He turned and hurried inside. When he returned, he was accompanied by a chubby man, dressed in an open-necked shirt and fawn-coloured trousers, who looked cool and relaxed. 'You're from the police?' said the chubby man.

'That's right.'

'I'm Guillermo López and I own the place. Always glad to give a hand.' He pulled out one of the free chairs and sat. The waiter put a bottle of Carlos I and two glasses, half filled with ice, down on the table. 'Have a brandy with me, Inspector?'

'I'll drink Carlos One with anyone.'

Lopez smiled. 'I was sure you'd appreciate it.' He poured out two large measures, pushed one glass across. 'Your very good health.' He raised his glass, drank. 'Now, I gather you've a problem?'

'I'm making a few inquiries. You'll know about the *Aphrodite* which sailed out on Tuesday and blew up out at sea?'

'You're on that case and not . . .' He cut the words short

and stared at the bottle of brandy with considerable resentment. If he'd realized that Alvarez was not professionally interested in certain financial aspects of the running of the café, he'd have served the same rough quality brandy that the tourists were given.

'It's beginning to look as if maybe there wasn't a gas leak and the cause of the explosion was a bomb, planted by terrorists. In which case, there's a chance that one or more of the terrorists was hanging around, making certain the boat did sail. So one of your waiters could have noticed him and he'll be able to give us some sort of a description.'

'D'you think they've time to stand around, looking at people?'

'It can't always be this busy.'

'Can't it?'

'Then you must be a rich man.'

López immediately showed caution. 'With the wages and social security payments the government forces me to pay? I'm lucky if I cover expenses.'

'My heart bleeds for you.'

'You work for the government, so you're all right.'

'Change jobs?'

Lopez said coldly: 'There's no way my blokes could have noticed anyone.'

'All right, on the face of things it does seem a bit unlikely, but a terrorist would have been under considerable tension and so he'd have been drawing attention to himself without ever realizing that fact. Don't forget the old saying, a guilty man can't stop smiling.'

López moved uneasily. It belatedly occurred to him that it had been a double mistake to serve Carlos I—not only was it a waste of very good brandy, but why would he have offered such a luxury unless he had something to hide?

'So what I'd like is to have a quick word with everyone who works here and ask 'em if they did notice anyone in particular.'

López longed to refuse, but accepted that to do so would be a bad tactical mistake. 'You'd best come through to the office.'

'Don't mind if I top the drink up first?'

'Take the bottle with you,' he replied bitterly.

CHAPTER 4

Alvarez felt quite cheerful when he drove out of Cala Vescari in the direction of the hills to the east and the reason wasn't entirely the quantity of excellent brandy he had drunk. His questioning of the staff at both the café and the Club Nautico had shown him to be right and Suau to have been wrong.

As the road began to rise, the land changed in character and became so rock-strewn as not to be worth cultivating; sheep and goats grazed the rough weed grasses, dried almost to the consistency of hay, and browsed on the bushes and the leaves of the lower branches of trees. Finally, the road levelled out and he found himself on a rough plateau, quite heavily wooded with evergreen oaks.

Back at the police station, they'd told him that Rullán lived down the first dirt track to the right once the road levelled off. He slowed, turned, and bounded along the pot-holed surface, his ancient Seat 600 protesting audibly.

The house came in sight just after he'd passed an oak which looked as if it had recently been struck by lightning. It was an old, small, boxy, one-floor place, still without running water or electricity, built by and for people whose only concern had been shelter; nevertheless, it possessed the attractiveness of simplicity. Beyond it were two outbuildings, in need of repair; one of them housed pigs. A number of chickens were working the ground, scratching, pecking, and scratching again.

As he braked to a halt, a small mongrel, curled tail held

high, came running up, yapping madly. He climbed out of
the car and the dog circled him. A man appeared around the
corner of the house and, limping slightly, walked towards
him; there was a lint and plaster patch on his right cheek and
much of his hair had been frizzled.

'Señor Rullán?'

'Well?'

'I am Inspector Alvarez of the Cuerpo General de Policía.
D'you mind if I have a word with you?'

'Isn't that what you're doing?'

Alvarez smiled. It warmed his heart to meet a true
Mallorquin. 'I think you had a word with Comisario Suau
yesterday?'

'If that's who that little shit was.'

Alvarez felt an even greater affinity with this ruggedly
built man, younger than himself, whose face beyond the
patch bore the mark of wind, rain, and sun.

Rullán shouted at the dog to shut up. Then he said: 'You'd
best come and sit down.' It was his way of saying that
although Alvarez was a self-confessed policeman, he didn't
appear to be a little shit.

Rullán led the way up to the house and then round the
side. The trees suddenly spread out to leave a cleared area
which reached to the edge of a cliff; beyond—and there had
been no previous hint of this—was a valley, a kilometre or
so wide; the far side of the valley was formed by rugged,
inhospitable hills, few of which had pines growing on them.
The sea lay to the right, the horizon over 30 kilometres away
because of the height at which they were.

Alvarez came to a sharp stop. 'My God, it's lovely!'

'You reckon?'

'Can't you see it is?' he said, almost angrily.

'And can't you see what's in front of your nose?'

'What d'you mean?'

'Walk on.'

Still not understanding, he walked on. Rullán's soul had

died, he thought; no matter how many times he'd stood and stared at such a view, had he had any soul he would still have caught his breath at the first fresh glimpse of such dramatic natural beauty . . . And then as he approached the edge of the cliff—but not too close because of his altophobia—he could look down at the floor of the valley and he saw roads, pylons, cranes, appartments, houses, shops, restaurants, and cafés, under construction and finished, ugly gashes in the earth where foundations had been dug and not yet filled, stacks of concrete blocks, piles of sand and aggregate, earth-movers, diggers, dump trucks, lorries, cars . . .

As the dog dashed backwards and forwards, chasing shadows, Rullán said: 'Five years ago, there was one house in the whole of the valley and Mad Magdalena lived in it. She owned the whole valley. And you could look up and see a pair of golden eagles, the last on the island, so they said, soaring up to the ceiling of the sky. Or you could watch a genet hunting or maybe a snipe jinking.'

'She sold out to the developers?'

'She didn't know what she was doing. And when she did begin to understand, it was too late.'

'Why didn't anyone try to stop what was happening?'

'Where d'you find men who close their ears to the chink of gold?'

'Didn't the authorities refuse permission to develop?'

'The mayor used to drive a Renault Five, now it's a BMW; the deputy mayor owns a flat in La Molina.'

Alvarez knew a bitter sadness; man's greed was the greatest destroyer of all.

'It won't go away, however hard you look,' said Rullán. He turned, to face the house. 'D'you feel like a drink?'

'If there's one going.'

They walked back across the open ground, hemmed in by the oaks, towards the house.

'Have you lived here long?' Alvarez asked.

'Since I was born; like my father.'

It was an isolated house now and would have been even more isolated in the old days of mule transport. Men had never lived in such isolation unless their faith had called upon them to do so or their job had demanded it. 'Was your father a charcoal-maker?'

'Like his father before him.'

In front of the house was a patio, shaded by two vines, which had a floor of hard packed earth. 'It's homemade wine,' said Rullán.

'There's nothing better.'

Rullán went into the house, pushing his way through a bead curtain. There were on the patio two aluminium-framed chairs—the only touch of modernity to be seen—and Alvarez sat on one of them. He settled back and his face was patterned by the sunlight which pierced the shield of vine leaves. There was a peace here which settled into a man's heart . . . until he remembered that two hundred metres away one could look down on a sight that pierced a man's heart. Could there never be beauty without ugliness, sanity without madness, courage without cowardice . . .

The dog jumped up on to his lap, startling him. He fondled its ears. Rullán returned, a glass tumbler in each hand. 'I've a brother-in-law who makes the wine—you'll find it's different from the stuff they sell in the shops.'

'It's none the worse for that.' Alvarez took one of the tumblers, drank. The wine was similar to that which he'd had when young and it evoked memories which seldom came to him now; of a house as primitive as this one, of working long hours in the fields while still virtually a child, of hunger that was never quite stilled except when a pig had been killed and there was, for a time, meat, sobrasada, butifarrones, negro, and chorizo . . .

'If the dog annoys you, turf her off.'

'It's fine. I like 'em.'

'She can be a bloody nuisance,' Rullán said, not quite concealing his affection for the dog.

Alvarez stared at the trees on his right. 'I don't suppose there's much charcoal made these days?'

'None in this part. I kept going with my old man when he was alive, but when he died that was that.' Rullán drank deeply, wiped his mouth with the back of his hand. 'There wasn't the sale for the stuff when the bottled gas came in.'

'So what did you do?'

'Worked wherever I could get work; on the land, in the fishing-boats, the hotels . . . I was three years a waiter at the Bahía.' He spoke scornfully. It was not difficult to understand that the scorn was directed at himself, a man who had been brought up in the luxury of solitude and independence, temporarily selling his labour in such a cause.

'I suppose you met Señor Todd at the hotel?'

'He used to stay there before he bought the house. One day, he asked me if I knew anything about boats. I told him, as much as the next man. So he said he was buying a boat and needed someone to look after her and was I interested?'

'Was it a full-time job?'

'No, but he was paying near enough a full-time wage.'

'Then he was a generous man?'

'When he reckoned generosity looked good.'

'It sounds as if you didn't much like him?'

Rullán shrugged his shoulders. 'He was a rich foreigner; it's not for me to like or dislike.'

'But you'll have had an opinion.'

'Aye.'

'Then what was your opinion of him?'

'Have you ever kept chickens?'

'Many years ago.'

'Then you'll remember there's always one cock who has to crow louder than the others.'

'And that one was him?'

'Right.'

'When did you first know you were going out on the *Aphrodite* on Tuesday?'

He shrugged his shoulders again. 'It could've been Saturday he told me.'

'Did you let anyone else know what was happening?'

'Why should I do that?'

Rullán, Alvarez thought, was a man who would never volunteer information to anyone. 'When did you go aboard on Tuesday?'

'It'd be just after eight.'

'Were there signs of anyone having been aboard during the night?'

'Everything was as it should be.'

'No smell of gas?'

Rullán said contemptuously: 'D'you think I'd not have done something about it if there had been? Anyway, there was an alarm for leaking gas and that wasn't sounding off.'

'During the morning, did you notice anyone ashore who was taking an unusual interest in the boat?'

'I'd too much to do to worry about ashore. The señor liked everything shipshape, especially if there was women coming aboard and I didn't know if there was or wasn't.'

'Did he often entertain women?'

'Does a dog chase a bitch on heat?'

'Like that, was he?'

Rullán finished his drink. He held out his left hand. 'The barrel's not empty yet.'

'I don't know that I ought to have any more. I had a brandy or two just before coming out here.'

'A couple of brandies and you're worrying?'

'So would you be if you'd seen the size of 'em.' Nevertheless, Alvarez handed him the tumbler.

Rullán took the tumblers into the house and refilled them, returned and sat.

'What d'you remember about things just before the explosion?' Alvarez asked.

Rullán drank then put the tumbler down on the ground at his side. The dog jumped off Alvarez's lap and went across;

Rullán stroked it in an abstracted way. 'They were eating.
The señor was too grand to serve 'em, so I had to. I'd put the
boat on automatic pilot, but I was worried because I'd been
off the bridge for too long. Then one of 'em couldn't decide
what cheese he wanted and so I left 'em to it. Back on the
bridge everything was all right and the only other vessel in
sight was still the fishing-boat half hull down on our quarter,
so I was about to go below again and see if the stupid bastard
had decided which cheese he'd eat when I noticed an Irish
pennant right for'd . . .'

'A what?'

'A bit of rag, caught up against one of the fo'c's'le rails,' he
answered, scornful of such ignorance. 'I went for'd and was
clearing that when the boat exploded.'

'You knew it was an explosion?'

'I knew something had happened, didn't I, seeing as I
found myself in the water, feeling liked I'd been kicked by
someone in hob-nailed boots?'

'Was there much of the boat left?'

'It had split in two. Pretty soon, the bows drifted away and
the after section sank. I swam after the bows, hoping to hang
on to 'em, but just before I reached them, they went under as
well.'

'Did you hear Señor each shouting for help?'

'I couldn't hear a thing except the bloody row in my
ears from the explosion that was like a chain-saw going
berserk.'

'And you didn't see him?'

'I'd have gone over if I had done . . . It's not like swimming
off the beach, you know. The sea was calm, but there was a
swell; didn't look much from above, maybe, but down in it, it
was enough to stop one seeing anything except when up on a
crest.'

'Are you a strong swimmer?'

'Strong enough.'

'How would you describe Señor Leach?'

'He's a nobody.'

'D'you actually know much about him?'

'What's there to know about that sort of a man?'

'And Señor Kendall?'

Rullán stopped fondling the dog's ears; she looked up at him, wagged her curly tail several times, then jumped up on to his lap.

'What kind of a man was Señor Kendall?'

'I heard you the first time. I don't know, and that's as straight an answer as I can give . . . Speak to him and he was all smiles and friendly; not like the señor who never let me forget he was paying me. And yet . . . Let's put it this way, I'd sooner have trusted Señor Todd than him.' He looked across. 'But let's get one thing straight. I never learned anything against him. All I'm saying is, I had a feeling about him.'

'A point of interest, he lived near where I do, but down in the port; Puerto Llueso.'

'Then he *was* crooked.'

Alvarez smiled. It was traditional for the inhabitants of each town to believe those from other towns were untrustworthy. Traditions died hard on the island. He noticed that the light had changed and softened, which meant that before long it would be dark. He finished his drink. 'I'd better start off for home.' He stood. 'Thanks for the wine . . . I'd say you're lucky to be living here, even if they are ruining everything in the valley; at least you can't see what's going on until you're up near the edge of the land.'

'There's luck and luck.'

'What's that mean?'

'It's lonely up here if you weren't born to it.'

There had been no missing the sudden, sharp note of pain in Rullán's voice. Alvarez remembered that although there had been mention of a brother-in-law, there had been none of his wife. 'Have you ever thought of moving?'

'Me?' Rullán seemed surprised by the question. 'Why should I want to do that?' he asked roughly.

Alvarez imagined the picture. A wife who'd lived with the solitude until the time when she'd looked below and had seen the beginning of the development and in her imagination she had endowed that development with a life of rich gaiety and happiness; and the more she imagined, the harder it had become to suffer the imprisonment of the solitude . . . And one day it had become all together too difficult . . . He sighed. One half of the world longed for what the other half rejected.

As Alvarez entered the house, Dolores came hurrying into the front room. She said breathlessly, her voice high: 'Have you had a crash?'

'Good heavens, no.'

'Then what's wrong?'

'Nothing. Why should anything be?'

'You can ask that when you come back so late I was certain you were dead?' Her distress was quickly turning into anger. 'Why didn't you ring and say you weren't dead?'

He thought of a humorous reply, but had the good sense to keep it to himself.

'I suppose you realize the meal is ruined?' She rested her hands on her hips and held her chin high; she was always a striking figure, with strong features and black, glossy hair drawn tightly down on either side of her shapely head; now her anger was adding a sense of commanding arrogance.

'You ought to have started without me,' he said in a placatory tone.

'And you think I could have eaten a single mouthful, thinking you dead?'

'I'm very sorry . . .'

'Does that repair the meal; does that unburn all the things that have burned?'

'The thing is, I had to go to Cala Vescari . . .'

'That's right outside your department. Why d'you go there? A woman?'

'That I should be so lucky!'

'So it's all just a joke for you?'

'Dolores, the superior chief phoned this morning and ordered me to go to Santa Vescari and work under Comisario Suau, who comes from the Peninsula. Suau has had me slaving flat out all day, right up until I left; from the moment I reported to him, I haven't had a single second's peace. He even refused to stop work for lunch.'

'You've not eaten all day?' she said, in tones of horror.

'Only a couple of sandwiches, which were quite horrible.'

'Then why are you just standing there, like a fool, instead of hurrying through for supper?'

In the dining-room, which was also the family sitting-room, Isabel, Juan and Jaime, were watching television. Jaime looked up. 'Where the hell have you been?' he asked sourly. 'We've been waiting grub until my stomach reckons my mouth's been kicked to death.'

'Just be quiet,' snapped Dolores. 'All the time you've been sitting here, doing nothing but drinking and complaining, poor Enrique has been working himself to death.'

'I'll believe that when I see his dead body.'

'Don't you dare say something like that.'

As he usually did, Jaime retreated before his wife's belligerence. He might be a Spaniard, but he did like a peaceful life.

'Well,' she snapped, 'are you now so lazy you can't even get him a drink?'

He watched her sweep through to the kitchen. Suggesting that either of them had a drink, when normally she did nothing but condemn them for their sottishness! . . . 'What d'you want, then—a coñac?'

Juan said, in his high-pitched voice which would soon break: 'I can't hear the telly with all this talking.'

Jaime, delighted to have the chance to vent some of his bewildered annoyance, informed his son that if there were one more word out of him, the television would be switched off. He half filled a tumbler with brandy and passed it across to Alvarez, looked at the kitchen door, saw it was closed and poured himself another drink.

Alvarez sat and stretched out his legs. He knew a deep contentment. In his hand was a drink and soon Dolores would dish a delicious meal that would undoubtedly prove not to have been ruined. What more could a man ask of life?

CHAPTER 5

Suau, standing by the side of his desk, used his right hand to slide back the sleeve of his light grey jacket so that he could look at his slim wristwatch. 'It is a quarter to ten.'

'Is it as much as that?' said Alvarez, faintly surprised.

'My final order to you last night was that you were to report here by eight this morning.'

'I know, but my cousin—actually, she's not really a cousin because my mother wasn't her mother's . . .'

'I regret I do not have the time to listen to a discourse on your antecedents.'

'No, of course not. Only I live with her and her family and she thought I looked so tired last night that she decided to let me have a lie-in this morning. So she deliberately didn't wake me up after the alarm went off.'

'After?'

'Yes, señor.'

'You need to be awakened after an alarm has sounded?' Suau walked over to the window, hands clasped behind his back, and stared out at the street below. 'Inspector, if I were asked to name one quality that distinguishes the man with initiative, drive, and an ability to succeed, I would name enthusiasm for his job. Regrettably, I have yet to discern any such enthusiasm in you.' He turned and walked over to the desk, his stride brisk, measured, and cocky. He picked up a sheet of paper, read what was typed on it, put the paper down. 'Superior Chief Salas telephoned me earlier on.' His voice rose. 'The murder of Señor Todd is continuing to be given very extensive media coverage in Britain and regrettably, more than one ignorant and biased commentator has cast doubts on our ability to handle the case. We have even been referred to as sleepy and incompetent.' He sat, so abruptly that the chair creaked as his weight came on it. 'Superior Chief Salas pointed out that the honour of the force now rests in our hands. I told him, 'Señor, have no fear. We shall uphold the honour of Spain, the honour of the Cuerpo General de Policía, and the honour of ourselves. If the case demands we work twenty-four hours a day, we shall work twenty-four; if it demands that we totally exhaust ourselves, we shall totally exhaust ourselves. You may rely on us.' . . . Do you understand that from now on we are going to eat, sleep, and drink this case?'

It seemed Alvarez was expected to say something. 'Yes, señor.'

'That no sacrifice can be considered too great?'

'No, none.'

Suau pursed his lips as if about to say that the last answer was unsatisfactory, but after a moment he changed the conversation. 'Did you question all the waiters at the café and the Club Nautico?'

'Yes, I did.'

'With what results?'

'None of them saw anyone suspicious.'

'Question them again.'

'But señor . . .'

'What did Rullán tell you?'

'He didn't notice anyone hanging about the boat on Tuesday and there wasn't the slightest smell of gas. Beyond that he couldn't really help us because . . .'

'Question him again. Have you sent the wreckage recovered from the boat to Palma?'

'When I saw the harbourmaster, the search boat hadn't

returned and he couldn't say when it would, so I carried on up to Rullán's place.'

'Surely you went back to the harbourmaster after questioning Rullán?'

'It was too late by then.'

'Too late for what?'

'He'd have gone home.'

'It didn't occur to you to find out where he lived?'

The man was mad, Alvarez thought.

'You will go now and find out what wreckage has been recovered and send this to the laboratory in Palma. You will again question the people I have mentioned and this time be more thorough; you will also question the staff of all the local hotels and find out the names of everyone who booked out on Monday or Tuesday—all names to be checked. You will visit shops, bars, and restaurants, and discover whether there has been anyone making inquiries about Señor Todd . . . Did Señor Todd employ any staff apart from Rullán?'

'I don't know, señor.'

'You should do. Find out and question any such staff. Get in touch with every quarry on the island and discover if any of them is missing explosives. Ring Interpol to ask for information on the organization which calls itself The Shining Sword of Allah; also ask them for a list of terrorists whose present whereabouts are unknown. Is there anything else you can suggest you should do?'

'No, nothing,' Alvarez replied dolefully.

The harbourmaster, seated at his desk, was having an argument with an Englishman. Since he spoke virtually no English and the Englishman spoke no Spanish, it was not a constructive argument. 'Here, do you speak any English?' the harbourmaster asked, as Alvarez stepped into the office.

'A little.'

'Then for the love of charity, find out for me what this chap's so steamed up about.'

The Englishman was large and loose-limbed and wore casual yachting clothes; his face and forearms were red from sunburn. 'Yes, I will bloody well tell you what the trouble is. I'm just out from home, right? I go to my moorings to see everything's ready for me to launch my boat and I find a Dutch yacht tied up there. So I come in here and ask what's going on and eventually the message seems to get through and so he says that tomorrow the berth will be free. Then I was having a coffee at a café half an hour ago and along walks the skipper of the Dutch yacht and we get talking and he says he's been paying a thousand pesetas a night for my mooring. So all that he's paid is owing to me. But can I get this bloke to understand?' The Englishman thrust out his chin. 'It's not so much the money as the principle.'

Alvarez spoke to the harbourmaster, then to the Englishman again. 'There is a rule that if a berth is empty, the harbourmaster may direct a visiting boat to it.'

'Fair enough. But what about the money?'

'There is another rule that the money belongs to the harbourmaster's office.'

'I wasn't told anything about this when I paid a million for the berth.'

'I am sorry. But those are the rules.'

'And my bad luck!' The Englishman glared at each of them in turn, stamped off out of the office, slamming the door behind himself.

The harbourmaster said, more in sorrow than anger: 'The English are often not at all well mannered.'

'Tell me something, who makes the rules?'

'I do, as harbourmaster.'

'And you alone represent the harbourmaster's office?'

'Yes.'

'So all the harbour dues come to you? . . . As I said before, it must be a pleasant job.'

'It has its compensations.'

Alvarez looked out through the window. 'Did the fishing-boat find any wreckage from the *Aphrodite*?'

'Vicente hadn't returned by the time I left last night and this morning I've been very busy, so I don't know.'

'Where d'you think I'll find him?'

'Like as not, at the boats. Either that or in a bar.'

Alvarez left the office and walked along to the end of the harbour. Half a dozen boats, all open and equipped with powerful stern lights which worked from bottled gas, were tied up stern first. Ashore, four fishermen, sitting on boxes or small crates, were mending nets, their dexterity making the job look simple.

Alvarez introduced himself and asked if one of them was Vicente Carbonell. They continued working and did not bother to acknowledge his question. He waited. Many fishermen were part-time smugglers and therefore very reluctant to speak to any policeman.

Eventually, the man on the right, heavily built, his face the colour of mahogany, his blue eyes sharp, stopped work and looked up. 'Well?'

'It was you who picked up the two survivors from *Aphrodite* on Tuesday?'

As the police's interest did not lie in what cargoes other than fish they had landed recently, the men relaxed.

'What if it was me?'

'For one thing, I'd like a chat about what happened. Over a coñac.'

Since it was obvious that he was not going to be able to avoid the questioning, Carbonell put down the shuttle by the side of the upturned orange box, folded down the length of net on which he'd been working, stood. 'Where d'you want to go?'

'Somewhere where the tourists don't.'

For the first time, there was a brief suggestion of approval in Carbonell's manner. He jammed his hands into the pockets of his heavily stained canvas trousers and, not speaking, led the way along back streets to a small, dimly lit bar whose floor was sanded. Alvarez ordered two brandies and after passing the glasses across, the barman stood around, making no secret of the fact that he intended listening to what was said.

Alvarez offered a cigarette, which was refused, lit one for himself. 'Did you actually see the *Aphrodite* blow up?'

Carbonell drained his glass and put it down on the bar. 'No.'

Alvarez signalled to the bartender, who refilled the glass. 'You can't say what colour the explosion was?'

'That's right, I can't.'

'So what first caught your attention?'

'The noise. What d'you think?'

'What did you see when you first looked?'

'Smoke.'

'You realized what had happened?'

Carbonell showed his contempt for the question.

'How long did it take you to sail over to where she'd gone down?'

'Half an hour, give or take.'

'Did either Rullán or the Englishman, Señor Leach, say anything when you rescued them about what had happened?'

The Englishman could do nothing but moan like a woman,' replied Carbonell contemptuously.

'And Félix Rullán?'

'What d'you expect a man to say at such a time?'

'Not much, but when he's shocked he may say something which later on he doesn't remember saying. I'm trying to find out what caused the explosion and if either of them mentioned anything particular about it which might help the experts.'

'It was gas.'

'There was no smell of gas earlier and there was an automatic alarm which didn't go off.'

'There was a boat in the harbour caught fire last year,' said the bartender, 'and that was gas. It's tricky stuff. Look at the woman in the block of flats in the Calle Escursach who was killed when a bottle exploded.'

Carbonell finished his second drink.

'Did you find any wreckage yesterday?' Alvarez asked.

'A lifebuoy and a bit of the upperworks,' replied Carbonell.

'Where are they?'

'Where d'you think? In the boat.'

And almost certainly they'd been there all night. Alvarez wondered what Suau would say if he ever learned how carelessly this important evidence had been treated. 'We'd better go and collect the bits. I've got to send them off to the experts.'

Surlily, Carbonell said that his home was nearby and he needed to fetch something from there first. Since there was no invitation to accompany him, Alvarez remained in the bar.

'Not one of your cheerful blokes!' said the bartender. 'Hardly ever see him smile. It's a funny thing, but he's got those very light blue eyes and so's my brother-in-law and he's as mournful as a brace of undertakers. Bit of coincidence, really. The world's full of coincidences. Take my other brother-in-law—and you're welcome to him! Last month he went to Palma and was having tapas in a bar and he got talking to another man and it turned out they'd been to school together. What were the odds against that?'

'I've no idea.'

'Or, for that much, it being Vicente who did the rescue? You can tell me coincidences don't happen very often, but I'll tell you, they never stop. A friend of my wife lost her wedding ring in the garden. Naturally, she searched and searched for it, but she couldn't find it and was proper upset. Then, two weeks later, she was in the garden again and dropped a clothes peg and went to pick it up and there was the ring! And I've another friend . . .'

Alvarez interrupted the loquacious bartender. 'Have you

any idea how far away Carbonell's house is?'

'Up the next street. Not much of a place, considering how well he's doing. Smartest fisherman on the coast. But to look at him, you'd never think he could put his hands on twice as many pesetas as most of us.'

'As far as I'm concerned, that still wouldn't add up to much.'

'You want to watch 'em come in here and spend. But have you ever heard a fisherman admit times are good? Maybe there aren't so many fish in the sea now, but there aren't a tenth of the boats chasing 'em. There used to be forty boats working from here alone and now there's not above half a dozen. Of course, that was when this was a fishing village and the nearest tourist was in Palma. Bit of a difference, and that's fact. And I suppose you can remember the old days just as clear as me?'

Alvarez was saved from the necessity of answering by the return of Carbonell who looked into the bar, his expression every bit as surly as before. He withdrew without speaking. Alvarez paid for the brandies and left, followed by the bartender's description of Cala Vescari immediately after the Civil War . . .

Carbonell walked at a pace that quickly left Alvarez breathless and he stopped trying to keep up. Only this morning, he'd read in the paper of a jogger who'd collapsed and died while jogging . . . By the time he reached the fishermen, Carbonell was once more seated on the orange box, repairing the net. 'Which is your boat?' he asked.

Carbonell paused long enough to point to the last of the boats.

Alvarez walked along the quayside; he came to a halt by the boat. By the side of the midships wooden engine cover, there were a damaged lifebuoy, heavily stained, and a small section of twisted, painted aluminium that was attached to a length of wood. The stern gunwale lay a metre below the quayside and it should have been a simple task to scramble down on to the boat, but as absurd as this must seem to anyone who didn't suffer from altophobia, even that short distance tightened knots in his stomach. He turned, intending to ask Carbonell to fetch up the two bits of wreckage for him, but saw that the four fishermen were intently watching him and it was not difficult to guess that they were hoping he would do something ridiculous. Summoning up all his courage, he prepared to descend.

CHAPTER 6

A kilometre out from Cala Vescari, Todd's house, Ca'n Bast, stood on rising ground so that from it one had a view over the town and out to sea. It was a large, U-shaped bungalow and between the two 'wings' was a kidney shaped swimming pool. Alvarez pressed the front door bell. The rich, he thought, lived in a different world. And whilst the poor tried to console themselves with the thought that money often didn't buy happiness, any consolation they enjoyed was inevitably soured by the certainty that poverty never could.

The door was opened by a woman, nearing middle age, who was dressed in an apron over a neatly patterned cotton frock. At first nervous, in the face of his friendliness she soon relaxed and it was she who suggested that they went and sat out on the patio.

Four aluminium chairs were set around a bamboo and glass table, just within the shadow of the house, on the near-side of the pool. She hurried to explain that, not knowing what to do, she'd carried on as if Señor Todd were still alive; she stumbled over the explanation, afraid that he wouldn't understand her. He assured her that she'd acted very sensibly.

'You come to work every day?' he asked.

'When he stayed here; and on Sundays as well. He didn't like doing things for himself.'

'Did his wife come out often?'

'Only occasionally. She always says it's so boring out here because there's nothing to do. She's a very grand señora who dresses like a princess.'

'How often would you say he came out?'

'Three, four times a year maybe.'

'How did you get on with him?'

'He told me what to do and I did it.'

'Would you call him a friendly man?'

She was silent for a while, then she said: 'He was always polite.'

'Because he thought a man in his position should be rather than because he naturally wanted to be?'

She was surprised that he understood. She nodded. 'He was a cold man.'

'But not, I gather, when it came to women?'

She was glad that he had been the first to mention this. She was a woman of strong loyalties even towards a man who had never bothered to hide the fact that he saw her solely as the hired help. But since she enjoyed a gossip as much as the next person . . . 'I've never met a man like it before, especially him being married. It wasn't just one, it was a succession!' There had even been the occasion—and might she be struck dead if it was a lie—when he had entertained one woman in the afternoon and a different one in the evening.

'Were they all foreigners?'

She answered indignantly. 'Would a Mallorquin woman ever be so shameless?'

He warmed to her, even while recognizing that she was out-of-date. When they had both been young it was true that there had been ladies and there had been whores; but after the caudillo had died, all values had been allowed to change and now it was a rash man who claimed he could always distinguish between the two. 'Were his women residents or visitors?'

'Both, I think. I mean, I'm sure some of 'em live on the island, but others I've never seen before or since.'

'Do you know the names of any who are resident?'

She hesitated.

'Well, do you?'

She was old enough to have known the times when the police had been so powerful and so little accountable for their actions that anyone without relations or friends in high places had taken the greatest care not to antagonize them. 'Only one and that's because she lives here in Cala Vescari.'

'There's no call to be worried. No one else will know how I came to question her.'

She fidgeted with the corner of her apron. 'She's not been in this house for quite a time. But when she was here . . . She didn't worry about me knowing. She used to walk around almost naked. She even left her clothes in his bedroom.' Her voice expressed her sense of outrage at this lack of hypocrisy.

'What is her name?'

'Zoe Williams,' she answered, mispronouncing both words.

'Where does she live?'

'In the urbanización on the other side of the village, but I don't know the name of the house.'

'She's probably on the phone, so the name will be in the directory. Will you . . .' He stopped. He'd been about to ask her to look, but she might never have gone to school so that now she could neither read nor write and he didn't want to embarrass her. 'Will you get the telephone directory for me?'

She stood and went into the house. He stared at the scene before him—patio, pool, extensive garden that was watered regardless of cost, magnificent backdrop of sea and sky . . . Covetousness might be one of the deadly sins, but if one were mortal how could one avoid sinning?

She returned. He thumbed through the directory to Cala Vescari, checked down the list of subscribers. Señora Z.

Williams, Ca'n Orpoto. He made a note of the name. Then he continued to question the maid. Had the señor appeared to be at all upset before Tuesday? Had anything happened to make him annoyed or frightened? Had there been a telephone call which had obviously disturbed him? Had there been a caller who'd demanded to see him and whose visit had left him nervous? Had he ever mentioned any troubles or fears? Had he asked her to be cautious about who she let enter the house? Had he ever asked her if she'd seen anyone hanging around the place?

At the end of half an hour, Alvarez was reasonably certain there had been no discernible change in the rhythm of Todd's life in the week prior to Tuesday. But Suau would never be content solely with her evidence. Alvarez could hear him, his supercilious voice pointing out that she was not a sophisticated woman and probably not a very intelligent one either, and could easily have missed signs that another person would have picked up. If Todd had received a threat before his death, it was more than possible that this had been in writing. So his papers must be searched . . . Alvarez sighed. It was so pleasant out on the patio, playing the part of a rich man.

Ca'n Orpoto was in Ibizan style—arches, flat roofs, slabby chimneys—half-way up the gentle slope immediately outside the town. The land here was very rocky and although the owners of some of the other houses had, with suburban-Surrey zeal, imported soil and laid down lawns, built goldfish ponds, erected dinky little summer houses, and even introduced gnomes, Zoe Williams had had the common sense to work with the land and not against it and the rocks stood proud as part of the landscape and around them grew century plants, prickly pear cacti, oleander and cistus bushes.

He left his car by the foot of the steps and climbed up these to the front door. He sounded the bell and waited. He heard the sounds of heels clacking on a tiled floor, then the door was opened.

A man could meet ninety-nine women and he would admire them, but without inner heat. But then he met the hundredth and, even though less beautiful than many of the ninety-nine, the first sight of her lit fires of desire in his mind and body. She was not young, as witness the lines in her face and the slight thickening of her neck, and her features were irregular, especially her mouth which was too full. She wore a bikini, notable for its brevity, and this made it clear that she had a generously proportioned body . . .

'Well? D'you think you'll know me next time?'

'Señora Williams? I am Inspector Alvarez of the Cuerpo General de Policía. I am enquiring into the death of Señor Todd. May I speak with you?'

'You'd better come on in.' She held the door fully open.

The hall was alive with colour, with two wall hangings, a small carpet, and floor tiles, all in brillant shades which almost, but never quite, clashed with each other. Between the two hangings there was a large pen and ink drawing of a hunting leopard; there were only a few lines, yet these had been drawn by a master and the leopard epitomised sleek, silent, deadly power.

The sitting-room led directly off the hall and as he followed her through he thought that although it was contemporary wisdom that a bikini should be worn by a slender woman in the first flush of youth, only one as brief as hers could have done justice to the rippling magnificence of her bronzed flesh or to the mysteries which just, but only just, remained mysteries . . .

They carried on through the sitting-room, by way of French windows, out on to the patio beyond. This, because of the slope, had had to be dug out and the land was raised to the back and far side thus providing a sun trap which was protected from any but a southerly wind.

'I sunbathe here when I'm not down on the beach,' she

said. 'It's great charm is that it's not overlooked.'

Whether she had intended there to be any special significance to her words, he did not know; he only knew that
into his mind there flashed the picture of her preparing to
sun-bathe and, being hidden, easing herself out of those two
scraps of material . . .

'Would you like a drink?'

He jerked his thoughts back to reality. He answered that
he'd very much like a coñac with ice, but no soda. As she
returned to the house, he sat on one of three chairs set out
haphazardly near a table. Was he, he silently demanded
angrily, a seventeen year old in whom the sap rose at heady
strength, or was he a middle aged man who should have
learned to control his thoughts . . . ?

She returned, carrying a tray on which were two tall
glasses, already beginning to frost. She sat and each of her
movements was for him filled with sensually provocative
power. He was irresistibly reminded of the leopard in the
hall.

'Why come here to ask about Deiniol?' she said.

'Because I understand you knew him, señora.'

'In any particular sense?'

He didn't answer.

She smiled mockingly.

He said hurriedly: 'I am interested in finding out what
kind of a person Señor Todd really was.'

'Why should that matter?'

'It is not yet certain who or what caused the explosion and
so we have to investigate all aspects of the case.'

'The British aren't in any doubt that terrorists were
responsible.'

'Señora, it is we who are conducting the investigation.'

She laughed, her very full lips parting to show white, even
teeth. 'How wise not to rely on newspaper reports! When I
was divorced, Gerald nearly had apoplexy because they
made the details sound so much juicier than they really were.

But then he's so very conventional; a missionary outlook, you could say. I really don't know why I married him except that it's so much more satisfactory to be divorced from a rich than a poor man.'

'What kind of a man was Señor Todd?'

'I still don't see why that should matter.'

'If the explosion was not an accident, and was not set by terrorists, then we need to look for someone who had a motive to murder him—or, of course, one of the others. When one knows something about a man, one can hope to understand what might have been the motive for his murder . . . Do you imagine there was anyone who might have wished him dead?'

'Probably dozens.'

'Why d'you say that?'

'The supply of aggrieved husbands must be virtually endless.'

'Then he had many lady friends?'

She laughed loudly, leaning her head back so that the sun stroked the whole of her long, shapely neck. 'The last time I heard the words "lady friend" used for a casual lay was when I was in my cot.'

He was shocked.

'Dear me, have I upset you? You can't bear to hear a spade called a spade? But how else to describe the relationship he was always after? A sharp, short sexual frolic, to be determined by him at the first hint of boredom.' She drank. 'And now you're busy wondering in that very proper mind of yours whether I was one of his "lady friends".'

'Certainly not, señora.'

'Then why the hell aren't you? Am I that unattractive?'

'It's . . . it's none of my business.'

'How very boring for you.'

'Señora, will you please tell me about Señor Todd.'

'Frankly, I'd rather talk about you.'

'What kind of a man was he?'

'How can I explain him to you, when all I know is what kind of a man he was to me?'

'Then what kind of a man was he to you?'

'Very handsome and assured, witty, and when he could be bothered, perhaps the most dangerously attractive man I've ever met. He was also a liar, completely self-centred, and totally ammoral—which, of course, was why he was so successful a politician.'

'But if you understood all that . . .' He trailed off into silence.

'I'd been around the world too long not to recognize an absolute bastard when I met one. But he'd also been around long enough to know when a women might recognize him and that made him wary, because he was scared of being identified. And this created a challenge. I've never been able to resist a challenge . . . Do you understand now?'

'No, not really. But it doesn't matter . . .'

'Dear me, a detective for whom all the baser aspects of human nature remain a closed book? . . . I can't believe that. I think you're fibbing.' She rested her elbows on the table and leaned forward so that her full breasts strained at their scanty covering. 'Why are you fibbing?'

He forced himself to look away from her breasts.

'Do you know, I reckon you're not nearly as stolid and conventional as you're trying to make out.'

'Señora,' he said hoarsely, 'I am very stolid and exceedingly conventional.'

'You're challenging me to discover the truth, aren't you?'

'No. I was . . .'

'I never, ever, can resist a challenge.'

He hurriedly drained his glass. 'Thank you for your help, señora.'

'My name is Zoe.'

He stood.

'I know a man who once told me that Zoe sounded like purring; do you think it does?'

The purring of a leopard. 'If you will excuse me, I must go now.'

'A Spaniard in a hurry—that's a contradiction.'

'I am a Mallorquin.'

'Of course—how remiss of me. And how proudly you proclaim the fact. I like a man who's proud of his birthright. But, proud Mallorquin, don't rush away, sit down and have another drink.'

'Thank you, no.'

'A one-drink Mallorquin. Another contradiction.'

He pushed his chair to one side, stepped away from the table and, with great dignity, said goodbye. He began to walk towards the house, suddenly remembered that he'd forgotten to ask her one question and came to a stop.

'You are going to have that drink after all?'

'Will you please answer one more question, señora . . . ?'

'Zoe.'

'Do you know the names of any of the married ladies with whom Señor Todd has recently been friendly?'

'Don't you think that's rather an undiplomatic question to put to me? Or are you convinced I'll have kept an eagle's eye on him? You place me as the jealous, vindictive type?'

'Surely only when challenged?'

'Ah!' she exclaimed with amusement. 'So the man is not, after all, the unresponsive, stolid character he would have us believe. Then perhaps neither is he so conventional?'

'Do you know the names of any ladies?'

'I simply can't remember. But rest assured, if a name does come to mind I'll let you know. So now tell me how I'll be able to get in touch with you?'

'I'll give you the number of the office to ring, and if I'm not in . . .'

'Then naturally I shall ring again.'

'But all you have to do is leave the message . . .'

'I set the rules for the challenge, señor inspector who is so very formal that he will not even call me by my christian name.'

He gave her the office number, said goodbye for the second time, and left, conscious of her mocking smile and her shapely, bronzed, velvet body.

CHAPTER 7

Suau, seated behind his desk, looked up at Alvarez with scarcely concealed dislike. 'We have received a preliminary report from the forensic laboratory. The explosion on the boat was caused by an explosive of the dynamite family. We are thus now certain that we are not dealing with an accident, but with a deliberate act of murder.'

'I rather imagined that from the . . .' began Alvarez.

Suau interrupted him, his voice sharper than ever. 'There are quite enough difficulties to the case without adding those caused by your imagination.' He tapped on the desk with the fingers of his right hand. 'In view of the facts—and I hope it is not necessary to remind you what those are—we are even more justified at this stage in assuming that this was the work of terrorists. Yet on your own admission it is clear that you have just spent a considerable time interviewing this woman, Señora Williams. Why?'

'I thought that until quite certain, we ought to consider the possibility that the motive for the murders was a private one . . .'

'Inspector, when Superior Chief Salas informed me that he was detailing you to assist me, he warned me of two things. Can you suggest what those two things were?'

'Not really, no.'

'One, that you seemed to view each and every order as something to be circumvented if you could not simply ignore it; two, that there is not one single set of circumstances, no matter how simple, that you cannot confuse to the point of total chaos. Do you know what I replied? One, I make certain that my subordinates carry out their orders immediately and exactly; two, that when I am in charge of a case there is no confusion, let alone chaos.' He stopped drumming with his fingers. 'Earlier, I gave you certain orders. Do you remember what they were?'

'Yes, of course.'

'Then tell me—in what terms did I order you to question one of Señor Todd's past mistresses?'

'You didn't—not in so many words. But . . .'

'My orders are not given in so many words, they are exact; and being exact, they are to be carried out exactly.'

'It really didn't take all that long . . .'

'I believe I have told you before that I am not interested in excuses?'

Alvarez struggled to find words that would make sense to this bantam-cock from Bilbao. 'The thing is, I've so often found that a crime isn't as simple as it first appears. I suppose it's because people are concerned and they're never as logical as one imagines they will be, so there isn't logic in the facts. Because of this, it's never really a waste of time to get to know as much as possible about the people involved because they are the key to what happened . . .'

'I am not surprised that the superior chief chose to speak as he did; if I were to confess any surprise, it would be at the fact that he has been sufficiently lenient as to have left you in a position which carries authority, no matter how slight.' He rested his elbows on the desk, joined the fingers of his hands together, stared at Alvarez over the triangle so formed. 'A good detective quickly learns that one of the basic tenets of efficient detection is this—what appears to be reasonable and logical, probably is. No doubt, I need to explain that?'

'There's really no need . . .'

'Crime is seldom a pattern of complicated behaviour if the investigator first establishes his priorities and then does not, either from ignorance or stubborn perversity, introduce extraneous matters.'

'I do appreciate all that, but even if at the moment the case does seem straightforward, surely we oughtn't to lose sight of the fact that Señor Todd cuckolded a great number of husbands?'

'You are, then, convinced that the dead man's sexual habits were held to be of great significance by the terrorists?'

'I'm not saying that. I'm . . .'

'Good. Then we need not pursue the matter any further.' Suau separated his hands, lowered them, picked up a single sheet of paper. 'During your unnecessarily prolonged absence, a message came through from a quarry near Simyola. An amount of explosive is either missing or may be missing —I failed to understand which because the man I spoke to was incapable of making a coherent report. You are to go there now and ascertain whether there has, or has not, been a theft of explosive. If there has, you will ask exactly how much has gone and the specifications of the missing amount; you will then proceed to discover whether there are any signs of breaking and entering, when the loss was first noticed, and when the theft most probably occurred. Is that perfectly clear?'

'Yes, señor.'

'One last thing. I do not require you to conduct an investigation into the sexual peculiarities of any of the workers.'

Alvarez left.

The quarry was on the south-west side of one of the foothills of the Sierra de Affabia. Conical in shape, the hill was largely covered with pine trees and so the actual site of the quarry was starkly obvious. Several hundred metres from the work face, a crusher and grader had been set up and when these were working, as well as loaders and dump trucks, the noise and the dust were very considerable. The rock was light grey in colour and it fractured easily into small chips with rounded edges; it was used extensively to surface dirt tracks and, in the smaller grades, in the manufacture of concrete.

The manager was a man of rugged features and thickset build. He pointed to the small wooden shed, a dozen metres from where they stood, with a hand which lacked a middle finger. 'That's where we keep the stuff.'

They walked over. There was no special security defences and Alvarez was satisfied that he could have forced the single lock without trouble. 'You discovered the loss four days ago?'

'That's right.'

'But didn't report it to the police.'

The manager jammed his hands in the pockets of his heavy-duty twill trousers which he wore despite the heat. 'The thing is, Angel came and told me and I checked and found it looked like two sticks were missing. Only . . .'

Alvarez waited.

'Sometimes, there's ten things to do and only time to do nine of 'em.'

'What you're really saying is, records don't always get kept as they should be?'

'That's the way it goes,' agreed the manager. 'Every stick that goes in or out is supposed to be entered in the explosives book, of course, but when things are rushed . . . So maybe these two sticks weren't really missing but just hadn't been booked out and so it didn't seem right to start creating. But when we had the message from you lot about wanting information on missing explosives, I reckoned it was time to get on to you.'

'Putting it in a nutshell, you may have lost two sticks of dynamite, but you'll never be able to be certain.'

'That's right.'

Hardly, thought Alvarez, a report that would please the comisario. 'Who, apart from the chaps who work here, knows you keep explosive in that shed?'

'I can't answer that. Could be anyone. I mean, everyone

knows we use the stuff and so it's got to be kept somewhere.'

'What's it look like?'

'See for yourself.' The manager took a key from his pocket and unlocked the door. Inside, there were shelves to the left and on the bottom one were three wooden boxes, each reinforced with angle-iron, and marked with warnings about the danger of their contents. The manager lifted up the lid of the end box and brought out a stick, twenty centimetres long and two in diameter, sheathed in bright red. 'It's a new type of dynamite, more powerful than the old stuff we were using; more expensive per stick, but supposedly cheaper in the long run.'

'Are any detonators missing?'

'I had a feeling you'd be asking that.'

'It sounds as if you don't know?'

'To tell the truth, we've never found the time to get around to keeping a check on 'em.'

Even Alvarez was surprised by this admission of slackness.

The manager said bitterly: 'How was I to know anyone would be mad enough to want to pinch 'em and blow someone up?'

'Assume two sticks of dynamite and two detonators were taken, would they be enough to blow up a fairly large motor cruiser, twenty-six metres long?'

'They'd do that with no trouble at all; especially this new stuff.'

Alvarez thought for a moment, then said: 'Have you noticed any foreigners around the place recently?'

'I haven't, no.'

'Have any of the other blokes who work here?'

'I can't answer for them.'

'No, of course not. But ask around, will you, and if any of 'em did, give me a ring.'

'Sure.' The manager replaced the stick of dynamite in the box.

*

The telephone call from London came through to the office half an hour after Alvarez had left. Inspector Jennings said, his Spanish both fast and correct: 'We've just received a message through one of the news agencies that a spokesman for The Shining Sword of Allah is claiming responsibility for the death of Deiniol Todd. As usual, the spokesman added a whole load of jargon to explain the murder; very turgid stuff.'

'Was it a genuine call?' asked Suau.

'Now things get difficult! This organization hasn't previously operated in the UK as far as we know and so no code has ever been arranged that would authenticate any call they made. The speaker, apparently, definitely wasn't British and the listener tentatively identifies him as of Near East origin . . . But the word to remember there is "tentatively".

'I've checked back on the two previous incidents on the Continent in which it is known they were involved and on each occasion responsibility was claimed immediately. Here, we are faced with a delay of something like forty-eight hours. Another thing, the speaker several times referred to a yacht, but the craft that was blown up was, I believe, a motor cruiser.'

'Wouldn't they be the same thing to most people?'

'That's a matter of opinion—except to any true yachtsman!'

'So you believe the claim may be false?'

'Yes, I think that's a strong possibility. A genuine call from the organization, making a false claim—in other words, they were trying to gain propaganda kudos for an incident they'd only read about.'

After thanking Jenkins, Suau rang off. A man who allowed his quick temper to show when there was no one to observe it, he slammed his hand, open palm downwards, on the desk. Why couldn't the bloody fool have come to the obvious conclusion, instead of introducing fanciful doubts . . .

The telephone rang a second time.

'Suau,' said Superior Chief Salas pleasantly, 'I've been

wondering how the case is progressing?'

'I'm sorry not to have been in touch with you, señor, but we've been working flat out and I thought that was more important.'

'Quite correct. And I wouldn't be troubling you now except that I've just had the Minister of Justice on to me. He's very concerned that in a case which is receiving so much publicity, some of it hostile, in the United Kingdom that the Cuerpo General de Policía should be seen to be conducting the investigation with total competency.'

'You can assure him that it is.'

'You remember that the honour of Spain is in our hands?'

'Indeed, señor.'

'Have you proved beyond all question that the crime was the work of terrorists?'

Suau was silent for a few seconds, then he said: 'Not yet, no.'

Salas's tone became a shade less genial. 'That should not be a very difficult task.'

'The trouble is, señor, it does seem there's the possibility that the case isn't quite as straightforward as it at first appeared.'

'Suau, have you been so misguided as to allow yourself to be influenced by Alvarez?'

'Of course not . . .'

'Then just make certain you don't.'

'Señor, there was a telephone call just before yours . . .' But he was talking into a broken connexion. He replaced the receiver, then slammed his hand down on the desk a second time.

Alvarez reported to Suau on his return from the quarry. Suau stood, walked round his desk, crossed to the window and stared out, hands clasped behind his back. He cleared his throat. 'I have been considering the evidence,' he said at length. 'I have, after very careful thought, decided that we

should broaden our investigations. It is essential that we
keep our minds open to all possiblities. Is that clear?'

'Not, really, no, señor.'

'While continuing primarily to treat this case as an act of
terrorism, we will not shut our eyes to alternatives; for
instance, we will consider the possibility that the motive may
not have been terrorism.' He cleared his throat a second
time. 'The competent detective is one who never allows his
mind to sleep, never reaches a conclusion until certain all the
facts are known, never hesitates to consider alternatives . . .
You will investigate the lives of the victims and discover
whether there exists a motive independent of terrorism for
the murder of any of them.'

'But when I told you I'd had a word with Señora Williams,
you said . . .'

'Please do not argue.' He unlocked his hands, turned,
walked back to his chair and sat. 'Well?'

'Well what, señor?'

'What are you waiting for? Question the friends and
relatives of the victims and discover whether there existed a
possible motive for the murder of any of them.'

Alvarez, looking even more lugubrious than usual, went
over to the door, opened this, but then paused. 'I don't
understand why . . .'

'There is no need for you to understand any more than
your orders.'

'Very well. I'll speak to Señora Kendall first of all.'

It was several minutes after Alvarez had left that Suau
remembered Kendall lived just outside Puerto Llueso. He
swore.

CHAPTER 8

For many years, Puerto Llueso had avoided suffering the kind of development which had ruined so many once beautiful stretches of coast. It had grown from the days when it had consisted of a few large houses on the front, belonging to wealthy Palma families who moved for the summer, and several fishermen's houses, but successive Llueso councillors had had the common sense to understand that small was lovely. Then something happened—and those who knew exactly what kept very quiet—and several major development plans were accepted and passed. Already, the port had begun to change in character and before very long the sprawl of houses and apartments would strip it of most, if not all, its previous charm. Greed had won yet another battle.

When Alvarez had first been posted at the Llueso department, the port had not begun to be spoiled so that now, every time he visited it, he knew regret and anger; regret that such a mistake could have been allowed, anger that those responsible would almost certainly never be called to account. He hoped that in hell the hottest corner was reserved for property developers.

Ca'n Ximo lay beyond the port, off the road which led across the narrow, beautiful, mountainous isthmus, still almost unmarked by man, to the Hotel Parelona. It was a large, two-storeyed house, set high off the ground, to avoid rising damp; unusually, instead of filling in the spaces between the foundations with earth, thereby inadvertently offering the damp a direct route upwards, these had been left open so that it was possible to crawl right under the house.

Alvarez climbed the steps up to the small front patio and rang the bell. The door was opened by a woman whom he knew and they chatted for a while before he said he wanted to speak to Señora Kendall.

'She's very upset,' she said doubtfully.

'I'm sure she is, but this is very important.'

'You'd better come in, then.'

The large sitting-room was attractively furnished with Spanish antiques as well as several modern, luxuriously comfortable armchairs, two Persian carpets, and several paintings of local scenes which bore the stamp of above-average ability.

Mrs Kendall was a tall woman, well built but not plump; she was dressed in a dark-coloured linen frock, around one arm of which was a black band. Her heavy, strongly featured face was made almost ugly by grief.

He said, with deep sincerity: 'Señora, I am very sorry to have to come here at such a sad time. Please understand that if it were not very necessary, I would not have done so.'

'Of course. Do sit down.' She spoke with a measure of forced calm.

He was nervous. Grief always upset him because all too easily he could imagine how the bereaved's thoughts were desperately seeking a falsity in what had happened; he had known this mental agony after Juana-María had died. 'Señora, although it seems that it was terrorists who blew up the boat, until we can be absolutely certain of this we have to check whether there might be another motive for the murder of anyone who was aboard the boat. So what I have to ask you now is whether you know of anyone who hated your husband sufficiently to wish him dead?'

From outside came the sounds of a rotovator working in one of the fields, its exhaust note rising and falling, while in sharp contrast there were the intermittent shouts of a man who was cultivating with a mule and a wooden and iron cultivator whose design had not altered in hundreds of years.

She suddenly said, her voice now shrill: 'That's a horrible thing to say.' She faced him, her dark brown eyes wild. 'How can you suggest anyone hated Arthur? When he did so much for people. Don't you understand . . .' She stopped.

Her lips were trembling and she was obviously having to use every last ounce of self-control to prevent herself breaking down. Had she been a Mallorquin, she would have given in to her grief before now, careless who saw her. He thought that the Mallorquin way was far kinder. 'Sometimes, señora, people don't behave or think rationally. The señor might have helped someone who resented being helped and in the sick mind there grew a bitter grudge . . .'

'Can't you understand, nobody could hate him?'

'He's not had a row with anyone in the past few weeks? Or received any threats?'

She shook her head as tears welled out of her eyes and began to slide down her cheeks.

He stood. 'I'm sorry to have caused you such distress.'

She stared up at him, hating him.

He left the sitting-room and quietly closed the door behind him; his last view of her was as she stared into a distance where she was alone.

As he approached the front door, the maid came out of the kitchen. He stopped, said quietly: 'Has she spoken to a doctor to see if he can help her?'

She shook her head. 'I've suggested it more than once, but she won't have anyone.'

'She needs help.'

'What can I do?'

'I suppose, nothing,' he answered sadly. He said goodbye and went out through the front doorway and down the steps to his car.

At the juncture with the Llueso road he turned left and this soon brought him to the front. Despite the hot-dog and ice-cream stands, the parked tourist buses, the shops filled with cheapjack mementoes, the restaurants and cafés, and the tourists, many of whom dressed without taste or decorum, the bay was a sight that never ceased to give him pleasure; there was here a beauty which man had not yet learned to destroy.

Near the front was an estate agent and he found room to park. He left the car and walked back, coming to a halt in front of the nearer of the advertising stands outside. Houses, flats, and fincas for sale. But all at prices beyond the comprehension of a mere inspector . . .

Seated behind the counter inside, on which were a number of pamphlets advertising one of the new urbanizacións being built, was a young woman who for the moment was more concerned with her appearance than with her work. She did not acknowledge his presence, but continued to paint her nails.

Is Señor Diego in?' he asked.

She finally looked up. 'He might be upstairs.'

'I'd like a word with him.' He waited. 'Perhaps it'll be easiest if I go up and find out?'

The sarcasm was wasted. 'Suit yourself,' she replied, as she inspected her other hand.

He was not, he decided, even within touching distance of the modern world; it bewildered, dismayed, and often angered him. A sure sign that he was growing old. He left the counter and climbed the steep stairs—the effort made him breathless; an even surer sign?—turned right on the very small landing, and went into the only room.

Diego was small and bouncy, possessed of an ebullient self-confidence which armoured him from any doubts about anything. 'Enrique, long time no see! I thought they must have locked you up.' He laughed as he shook hands; he had several gold fillings in his teeth and his smile was wide enough to put them all on display. 'Sit down and tell me what brings you here. But first of all, are you thirsty?' He answered his own question. 'Is a starving man hungry? What'll it be—coñac?' He went across to a corner cupboard and opened the door. 'As I always say, these are my best assistants.' He indicated the bottles inside. 'I wouldn't like to guess how many sales a couple of drinks have assisted.' He bent down and brought out a bottle and two glasses, half filled the glasses, passed one across. 'The client's hesitating, wondering whether he can possibly begin to afford to buy the property. I give him a couple of good strong drinks and he becomes twice the man and signs on the dotted line to prove it.'

'I'll remember that when I'm looking for a finca.'

'You don't think I'd work that way with an old pal like you? . . . And if you're looking for somewhere, I've just the place which isn't even on the books yet. Forty thousand square metres of prime land, a well that's never run dry, and a caseta that could be turned into a really nice, comfortable home without trouble. I'll let you have it for nine million and not take a peseta profit for the sake of old times.'

'You'll have to value the old times much higher than that before I can afford anything on your books.'

'Nine million? That's peanuts for these days.'

'Only to monkeys.'

'As sour as ever. Why don't you give your mouth a treat and smile?' He roared with laughter, settled behind the desk, raised his glass. 'Here's to us, then, and may our shadows never grow thinner.' He drank. 'So if you're not buying, what brings you here apart from wanting to see an old pal?'

'I reckoned you might be able to give me some information. You'll have heard about Señor Kendall being killed?'

'Of course. As I said to Rosalía when we saw the news on the telly, you never know when you've got it coming to you . . . So drink up and have another, just in case. It'd be terrible to reach those pearly gates and know you'd had time for one more but had turned the chance down.'

'I'm just come from seeing his wife.'

'Then you're near freezing.'

'Why d'you say that?'

'Why? She's the nearest thing you'll find to a walking icicle.'

'She's extremely distressed over his death.'

Diego was about to say something facetious when he noticed the expression on Alvarez's face; he checked the words.

'I want to know what kind of a man her husband was.'

'Why?' Diego's manner sharpened and there was now a wary expression in his eyes. It was not luck which had brought him success, as he usually claimed, but a very sharp intelligence.

'We're not certain the explosion was the work of terrorists, aiming to kill Señor Todd and careless of any other casualties.'

'Who else could it have been?'

'We don't know, which is why I'm asking around, trying to find out if there was a motive for the murder of any of the others. Señora Kendall told me that it's impossible anyone would ever have wanted to murder her husband because he was so liked. Would you confirm that?'

'Only if I were too tight to know what I was saying.'

'What's that mean?'

Diego drained his glass, stood. He held out his hand. 'Are you ready for the refill?'

Alvarez passed his glass across. 'Why should someone have disliked him?'

'Not someone; anyone who ever did business with him.' Diego went over to the corner cupboard and picked up the bottle. 'That man was one of the sharpest dealers around and if I were asked for an opinion, I'd say there must be a whole raft of people who shed tears of joy, not sorrow, at the news of his death. That man could have made a profit out of an Arab horse dealer.' He poured out two brandies.

'So what's the difference from other estate agents?'

'Do you mind? There are some of us who regard the relationship with the client as one of absolute trust; his

interests come before our own.' He returned, handed Alvarez
a glass, sat.

'Are you really saying that he swindled his clients?'

'That's dangerous talk, even when a man's dead. And
you've got to remember that swindle is a word which means
different things to different people. What you call good
business, I might call a swindle.'

'It's far more likely to be the other way around.'

'You like your little joke, don't you? . . . There are limits.'

'But who sets them?'

'That's something you might have asked him. Frankly,
I'm surprised he was never denounced. Especially as, being a
foreigner, he had an unfair advantage when dealing with
other foreigners because they instinctively trusted him. And
on top of that, he never did have a work permit. Yet none of
the other estate agents ever put the boot in.'

'I wonder you didn't, since it would have removed some of
the opposition.'

'Well, things weren't that simple. They never are.'

'He'd something on you?'

'You're not just sour, you're becoming nasty.'

'Call it the cynicism of age . . . Can you give me names of
people he swindled?'

'I wish you wouldn't keep using that word.'

'Jangles the nerves?'

'There's really only one I can give you because he's the
only one of whom I've first-hand knowledge. It was some
time back—four years, I guess—when he was still handling
any work that came his way and hadn't become too choosy
and grand for anything but the luxury trade. There was this
Englishman who hadn't much money and was looking for
somewhere cheap; his wife was an asthmatic and he hoped
she'd be fitter on the island. Kendall told him about a real
bargain—a caseta on four thousand square metres of land,
fronting the bay. Not being a complete fool, the Englishman
wanted to know why a property like that was going so

cheaply when everything else on the front cost a fortune. Kendall said the town hall had refused permission for the caseta to be restored and lived in, so the property didn't on the surface appear to be worth anything, but he knew the man who mattered in the town hall and if a hundred thousand pesetas were slipped in his direction, permission would be granted. What he didn't add was that the provincial authorities had declared the area a nature preserve and so it didn't matter what anyone in the town hall did or said, there could be no permission.

'The Englishman bought the property for three million and gave Kendall another hundred thousand to pass on to his contact in the town hall. A couple of months later, Kendall returned, handed back the hundred thousand, and said he was extremely sorry, but his contact had moved on and the new man was a fool who wasn't interested; all very bad luck, but he couldn't possibly have known such a thing was going to happen. The Englishman demanded his three million back, Kendall said he was even sorrier, but everything had been done in good faith and the money had been paid to the owner of the land who'd since left the island. That left the Englishman with some rubbishy land and a tumble-down caseta he wasn't allowed to restore and live in.'

'And he couldn't complain to the authorities because he'd been eager to be a party to bribery and corruption?'

'That's the way it played.'

'Did the Englishman threaten Kendall?'

'Can't blame him if he did, can you?'

'What's his name?'

'Sutherland.'

'Have you any idea where he lives now?'

'Here, in the port. As a matter of fact, when he had to rent somewhere because he'd not enough capital left even to buy a house in the village, he came to me and I found him a cheap flat.'

Alvarez drained his glass and put it down on the edge of the desk. 'Can you give me some more names?'

'As I said before, he's the only one I know about for certain.'

'Suppose I say I don't believe that?'

Diego smiled blandly.

'What have you got against Sutherland?'

'Why should I have anything against him?'

'Because you've named him and no one else, yet you've always got your nose so close to the ground that you could probably give me another dozen names if you wanted to.'

'You flatter me.'

'Not intentionally.'

Diego pulled open the small middle drawer of his desk and brought out a box of cigars. He offered a cigar, lit his own. 'You've had a lot to do with the English?'

'What if I have?'

'Then you'll know how they act towards us; they're either condescending or contemptuous.'

'And which was he?'

'Both. Yet he couldn't even afford to buy a village house.'

Alvarez stood. 'I hope to God I never get on the wrong side of you.'

CHAPTER 9

Calle Hermitage was at the back of the port and until recently it had been the last made-up road before the fields; now the fields had been engulfed by development. Quite apart from the noise of the building during the day, it was not a quiet area; the road was short, yet it contained two cafés and a restaurant and these were frequented by the kind of tourists who, after several drinks, seemed to feel under the compulsion to sing, with complete disharmony, until the early hours of the morning.

Even by the island's standards, the block of flats had been badly built. As was customary, having drawn up the plans and collected his very high fee, the architect had lost interest in the project and left all the unimportant matters, such as making certain that the plans and specifications were adhered to, to his aparejador. His aparejador had unfortunately been greedier than usual and in consequence the workmanship and the quality of the materials used had been even poorer than the architect would have imagined them to be, had the architect ever imagined them. Major cracks had appeared in the walls within eighteen months and the owner of one of the flats, a surveyor from Bristol who came out twice a year, had given it as his worried opinion that the foundations were shifting. Had he known just how few foundations there were to shift, he would have been ever more alarmed.

The lighting in the communal areas was not working and Alvarez had to climb the stairs in a gloom that was not quite deep enough to hide the flaking paint. He reached Flat 2c and knocked on the door. It was opened by a woman, older than he, whose face was drawn and, surprisingly in the middle of so searing a summer, pale. He introduced himself. Flustered, she said that her husband wasn't at home but was out doing the shopping because her asthma was so bad at the moment. But he'd be back soon and if Alvarez would like to wait . . .

A quarter of an hour after he had been shown into the small siting/dining-room, Alvarez heard Sutherland arrive. There was a murmur of voices from the hall, then the door opened and he stepped inside. He was a compactly built man, with a square face and leathery skin; there was a scar on his right cheek. He had a tightly clipped moustache, which he frequently fingered. He was dressed in shirt, shorts, and long socks, and these last added a touch of dated colonialism.

His manner was aggressive and his tone of voice hectoring. 'What's the trouble, then?'

It was small wonder that Diego had taken so sharp a dislike to him, Alvarez thought; or that his wife resembled a faded flower. 'I am investigating the death of Señor Kendall and I would like to ask you some questions.'

Sutherland walked over to the far wall, turned, and stood with his back to it, his thick, stubby hands jammed into his trouser pockets; it seemed as if in his mind's eye there was a fireplace behind him. 'I'm damned if I see why you've come here to bother me. Kendall was murdered by terrorists and I know nothing about those bastards except they ought to be hanged.'

'We cannot yet be certain that terrorists were responsible.'

'You lot are never certain about anything.'

'There are some things which suggest that perhaps this was not an act of terrorism and so I am having to check as many of the facts as possible.'

'What has . . .' Sutherland stopped as the door opened.

Mrs Sutherland stepped just inside the room. 'I was wondering if you'd like something?' she asked, in her diffident, breathless voice.

'There's no need,' replied Sutherland abruptly, not bothering to thank her. He waited until she'd withdrawn and shut the door, then said: 'I still don't understand why you've come to speak to me.'

'You knew Señor Kendall.'

'In what sense? If you mean socially, not bloody likely.'

'But you had met him, surely?'

'A few years back I learned the hard way that he was a bloody crook.'

'You are referring to the caseta he sold you, but for which you have been unable to get permission to renovate and enlarge?'

Sutherland showed his angry surprise. 'How d'you know about that?'

'I believe you were induced to pay considerably more for that property than it was worth?'

'Three million. And all he did was bloody laugh in my face when I threatened to take him to court to show him up for the crook he was.'

'You were resentful?'

'Resentful? Why don't you foreigners ever learn to speak English properly? Just resentful, when half my capital had been stolen?'

'Then you were much more than resentful?'

'I wasn't bloody laughing, that's for sure . . . The wife's asthma had got so bad the specialist in England had said that all he could suggest was that we tried living in another climate. So we decided to come out here and put together all our money which wasn't much because we'd lost a bundle . . .' He stopped and his mouth tightened. He fingered his moustache. 'But we'd still enough for those days to buy a small place out here. And when we saw the caseta, the wife fell in love with it and was so convinced she'd be better living in it that she started to get better then and there . . . And then that bastard swindled me out of the three million and we hadn't enough left to buy any property and the wife became so emotionally upset her asthma became really serious and she had to be rushed to hospital and damn near died . . .'

For the first time, Alvarez knew a measure of sympathy for this pugnacious, dislikable man. 'Did you threaten him because of what he'd done?'

'What d'you mean?'

'Did you threaten to get your own back?'

Sutherland thrust out his chin and spoke with added belligerence. 'Are you trying to bloody suggest I had anything to do with killing him?'

'At the moment, what I am doing is finding out whether you had cause.'

'I've had cause enough to get my own back on any number

of people, but that doesn't mean I've slaughtered 'em . . .
This all happened years ago.'

'Does that make a difference?'

'And you're supposed to be the detective?'

'Time can make one hate harder, not forget . . . Did you
ever threaten to kill him?'

'I said I'd thrash him with a riding crop. That's what one
does with crooks.'

'When one's not in a position to take them to court?'

Sutherland's face darkened.

'Did you ever physically attack him?'

'No.'

'Why not?'

'Because . . . because the wife made me promise not to, if
you must bloody know. She can't stand a scene and when she
gets emotionally upset, her asthma's much worse.' He
brought his hands out of his pockets, stamped over to a small
table on which was a cigarette case, opened this and brought
out a cigarette which he lit. It was impossible to judge
whether his failure to offer Alvarez one was due to forget-
fulness or was deliberate.

'When did you retire from work?'

'What's that to you?'

'Please answer the question.'

It was obvious that the sharp change of subject perplexed
Sutherland. He looked quickly at Alvarez, then stared at the
rising smoke of the cigarette. Finally, he said: 'I retired just
before we came out here. I finished early because of the
wife.'

'What was your job?'

'Civil engineer.'

'Then you had to know about explosives?'

'Enough to be certain that the blokes using 'em were
getting things right.' His voice again rose. 'What are you
getting at now?'

'I am merely trying to assemble all the facts.'

'"Assemble all the facts". What's that from—some bloody phrase book? . . . Just try and get this into your head. If I'd decided to kill the bastard, I'd have done it a long time ago.'

'Do you have a residencia?'

'What if I do?'

'May I have it, please?'

'Why?'

'I intend to have the photograph copied.'

Sutherland looked as if about to argue vehemently, but abruptly he left the room, returning quickly and aggressively handing over a two-year residencia. Alvarez thanked him for his help and said goodbye. He made no answer. Alvarez crossed to the door and went out into the tiny entrance hall. Mrs Sutherland stood just inside a passage and he did not doubt that she had been listening to what had been said. Her expression was strained and frightened and she looked ill; he could hear the difficulty with which she was now breathing. Sadly he thought, not for the first time, that the bitter consequences of a crime were seldom restricted to criminal and victim.

At home, Jaime was in the dining-room. 'There've been two telephone calls for you.'

Alvarez sat down on the nearest chair and wished he could free his mind of the pale, strained face of Señora Sutherland.

'One, ten minutes ago, was from someone called Suau; speaks with a funny accent.'

'That's my comisario; he comes from Bilbao.'

'The one who's throwing his weight around?'

'That's him.'

Jaime opened the cupboard and brought out a bottle of brandy and two glasses. 'Bloody foreigner,' he said, meaning a Spaniard who came from beyond the island.

'What did he want?'

'To talk to you. Demanded to know where you'd been all

morning. I said I didn't know anything except you'd left the
house just before seven.'

Alvarez smiled briefly. 'I doubt he swallowed that . . .
Who was the other call from?'

'I wouldn't know. It came through before I got back and
Dolores took it; she just told me about it.' He poured out two
drinks, handed one glass to Alvarez, then sat.

'Is there any ice?'

'Only in the fridge. And she's busy getting lunch.'

When Dolores prepared a meal, it was far better not to
disturb her; she could be very temperamental, especially if
things were not going as she wanted. But it was very hot and
his throat was drier than the Sahara. He came to his feet. 'I'll
go through and get some.'

'Good idea,' said Jaime approvingly, happy that it was not
he who was being called upon to test his wife's temperament.

Despite the fact that the extractor fan above the stove and
a free-standing fan on one of the working surfaces were
switched on, the kitchen was like an oven and Dolores,
working at the stove, was perspiring freely. 'What do you
want?' she demanded belligerently.

'Just a little ice.'

'So you're drinking again?'

'It is the first today.'

'I'd have to be a fool to believe that.' She stirred the
contents of an earthenware pot. 'Then hurry up and get it
and clear out of here.'

He went over to the refrigerator, opened the ice compart-
ment, and brought out one of the rubber trays of ice. He
started back to the doorway into the dining-room.

'There was a call for you earlier on.'

He came to a halt.

'It interrupted me when I was making the soup. If the
soup's ruined, it won't be my fault.'

'I'm very sorry.'

'And does that help repair the soup?' She turned round,

picked up a sprig of wild marjoram from the table, turned back and very carefully shredded a few leaves into the pot.

'I'll bet it tastes as delicious as ever.'

She made a sound which signified contempt for such obvious flattery—but she did agree with the sentiment. 'The call was from a woman; a foreign woman,' she added very disapprovingly. 'Her Spanish was atrocious.'

He was surprised. 'Who on earth was it?'

'She said her name was Señora Williams.' Her tone suggested that she would not have been surprised to discover that this was a lie.

'But how did she ever find this number?'

Dolores sniffed. Men, more especially older men, were such fools. He'd obviously given this woman his telephone number and had been waiting on tenterhooks for her to ring, yet now he was weakly trying to make out that the call had come as a complete surprise.

'Did she say what she wanted?'

'You're to ring her back; the number's on the pad.'

'She didn't give any hint . . .'

'I was far too busy to speak to a foreign woman.'

He returned to the dining-room, dropped several ice cubes into his glass and then passed the tray to Jaime. He had a quick drink, went through to the front room. Zoe's number, in the somewhat childish, elongated handwriting of Dolores, spread right across the top page of the pad. He dialled the number. 'This is Inspector Alvarez. You asked me to ring you, señora?'

'What a terrible memory you have.'

'How do you mean?'

'I told you to call me Zoe.'

'Yes, but . . .'

'And I refuse to call you Inspector. You might be an inspector of drains. What is your Christian name?'

'That really doesn't matter . . .'

'Christian names are critical. I could never adore a

Percival or Cecil; I like my men to be made of much sterner
stuff. So what's your name? Or are you now too embarrassed
to tell me in case it reminds me of Clarence who insisted on
treating me as sweet sixteen when I was longing to
become sour seventeen?'

'Enrique.'

'Good. That's a name of determination.'

'How did you find my telephone number?'

'Simple. I telephoned the one you gave me and spoke to
some horrid little man and asked for it.'

'That . . . that wasn't Comisario Suau?'

'I've no idea what his name was. Zachary something or
other, from the sound of him . . . Enrique, you must come
and see me this afternoon.'

'Why?'

'He says why! . . . I'm beginning to adore you, completely
and utterly. If I said to any other man to come and see me
this afternoon, he'd come running. It's no wonder I find your
challenge quite irresistible.'

'I am not challenging you, señora.'

'Every time you say señora instead of Zoe, it's a subtle
challenge.'

'Certainly not.'

'Then say Zoe.'

He remained silent.

She chuckled. 'This afternoon. It's very important.'

'Tell me what you want now.'

'Let your imagination roam. Just as far as it can.' She cut
the connection.

His imagination roamed.

When he returned to the dining-room, Jaime looked
curiously at him. 'You're sweating as if you'd been running
hard.'

But could he run hard enough? he wondered.

CHAPTER 10

Stretching for kilometres on either side of Palma were hotels, flats, houses, shops, restaurants, and cafés, squeezed together as closely as lax zoning laws and ingenuity allowed. The sea, once crystal clear, was at times nearly opaque from pollution and the beaches all but disappeared from the press of bodies; the air stank of exhaust fumes where once it had quivered to the tingling scent of wild herbs . . .

Alvarez parked his car, climbed out on to the pavement, and felt sweat break out as the heat, trapped by the high buildings, closed in on him. The traffic was constant and there were so many pedestrians that they spilled off the pavements on to the roads. A straggling group of men, wine bottles in their hands, shouting inanely, pushed past him, careless that he all but lost his balance. For him this, and not the traditional scene of brimstone and fire, was hell. Fire cleansed.

He entered the tall block of flats. The single lift was out of order and on its walls was a wealth of graffiti, mostly in English, all of it obscene. He climbed the stairs. On the bare concrete of each landing there was a litter of empty bottles, glass and plastic, ice-cream wrappers, and used cartons from the rapidly burgeoning fast food stores.

The Streets were both in their early sixties; he was tall and thin, she was short and plump; he spoke slowly and with reserve, she spoke quickly and with open warmth; he did not rush to make Alvarez welcome, she was immediately friendly.

They sat out on the small balcony off the sitting-room, shaded by the building. Street picked up a briar pipe and worn leather pouch and began to tamp tobacco into the bowl. 'You need to understand one thing, we aren't close friends of Cyril Leach's.'

'But we do get on well with him,' said Madge.

'That's hardly the same thing.'

'I don't know what the difference is in practical terms.'

'Of course you do.' He put the pouch down and picked up a box of matches.

She turned to Alvarez. 'Ken is one of those irritating men who really enjoys arguing. It doesn't matter what you say, he'll hold the opposite just to be provoking and even if he knows he's talking nonsense. I can't think why I haven't divorced him on the grounds of social sabotage.'

'Stop complaining. You know you could never find anyone else half as perfect.'

'Listen to him!'

Alvarez smiled politely. They were, he thought, two people who'd learned to enjoy their differences and make of them something which drew them closer together. 'But you do, at any rate, know him well enough to tell me something about him?'

'If you can give us a good reason why we should.' Street struck a match and sucked flame into the bowl. His wife looked at him, worried by his answer.

'Señor, as I explained at the beginning, there are many things in this case about which we cannot yet be certain. If it was an act of terrorism, aimed at killing Señor Todd, how did the terrorists know when the boat would be sailing? If it wasn't and the motive was quite different, what was that motive? Once we can discover that, it will be much easier to identify the murderer.'

'All right. We'll help you if we can.'

'Thank you . . . I think that Señor Leach had drinks with you on Sunday?'

Street looked vaguely surprised. 'Was it only then?'

'That's right, dear,' said his wife. 'And the Azells were meant to come as well, but Felicity rang up to say Mike had a sore throat.'

'While he was here,' said Alvarez, 'Señor Leach told you about the boat trip?'

'Couldn't get the news out quickly enough to try and impress us,' replied Street.

'You being perfectly beastly to poor Cyril,' she said.

'Even you have to admit he did go on and on about being invited by the great Deiniol Todd.'

'It was quite an event, I suppose.'

'That depends on what you think of Todd.'

'And what do you think, señor?' asked Alvarez.

'Wouldn't have lasted a day in our regiment.'

She chuckled. 'Don't you believe it. He'd have had the lot of you, including even old Colonel James, eating out of his hand. The trouble is, you're jealous of him.'

'And you can't see beyond that smooth charm.'

Her expression suddenly changed. 'Oh dear, we really shouldn't be talking about him like this since he's dead.'

'Until he's canonized, we can tell the truth.'

'But it's being so unfair. After all, we've only ever met him the once.'

'And have you forgotten how it was so difficult for him to lower himself sufficiently to reach our level?'

'I told you at the time, you were just being stupid about him and it was nothing to do with us. There was that very theatrical blonde on the other side of the room and we were very poor company in comparison.'

'You stick to your version, I'll stick to mine.'

'Of course you will. You always do when it suits your prejudices.'

Street found that his pipe had gone out. He struck another match and the air was so still that the flame did not bend until he drew on the pipe.

'Did either of you tell anyone else that Señor Leach was going on this boat trip on Tuesday?' Alvarez asked.

'Why should we?' demanded Street. 'We aren't the kind of people to try to gain social prestige by boasting we know someone who breaks bread with the great Deiniol Todd.'

'The inspector wasn't suggesting we were,' she said worriedly.

Street suddenly laughed; a snorting, nasal laugh. 'I forgot, it's only the English who can be such bloody silly snobs.'

'Señor, I asked because sometimes one talks to people carelessly; perhaps you were speaking with someone about boats and mentioned that Señor Leach was going out for the day with Señor Todd?'

'And perhaps I wasn't. Other people's boats are almost as boring as other people's ailments.'

'Have you known Señor Leach for very long?'

She answered the question. 'Pretty well from when we first came out and that's over five years ago now. We were invited to a drinks party and he was there and no one seemed to be talking to him so I asked him how to go about doing something or other and he told me. Ever since then, we've seen quite a bit of him and he's always gone out of his way to be helpful.'

'Because he's lonely,' said Street.

'That's not a very nice thing to say.'

'You've often told me I'm not a very nice person.'

'Then try to change and think nice things of people.'

'I prefer to face facts.'

'Stop being such a cynic.'

'After thirty years in the army?'

Alvarez said: 'If you were in the army, señor, you will have learned to handle explosives?'

'Had to know something about them, of course. Why the interest? D'you think I blew up the boat?'

'For heaven's sake!' she exclaimed.

'If I'd done the job, I wouldn't have bungled it so that there were survivors.'

'Ken, stop talking like that. The inspector won't under-

stand your terrible sense of humour.' She turned to Alvarez.
'He's upset a lot of people out here.'

'Only because so many of them are hypocrites.'

Alvarez asked: 'Would you think that Señor Leach has
many enemies?'

Street answered. 'You need character before people dislike
you.'

'Ken, that's quite enough,' she snapped, 'more especially
when the poor man's badly hurt and still in hospital.'

He muttered something, but not loudly enough for either
of them to understand him. It was clear that there were limits
beyond which his wife would not let him go.

'You're being totally unfair to Cyril,' she continued.
'Maybe he is very quiet and uncertain of himself, but he's
kind and will help anyone in trouble. Just because he doesn't
push his own views belligerently and sometimes sounds a bit
. . . well, Uriah Heepish . . . doesn't mean he's characterless.
I'd rather go to him if I were in real trouble than I would a lot
of other people we know.'

'It sounds, señora,' Alvarez said, 'as if he's not the kind of
man to have rows with people?'

'He'll do anything in his power to avoid an embarrassing
situation.'

'He told me that his wife lives in England—have you met
her?'

'No, we haven't. And in fact it was some time after we first
met him that we learned he was married.'

'Does he have a lady friend?'

She looked at her husband and he became very interested
in his pipe and drew on it repeatedly so that smoke billowed
up. 'That's not a subject I like talking about,' she said finally.

'Nor do I, señora, but two men were murdered and he and
another were injured. It's my job to find out who was the
murderer and I may not be able to do that until I've learned
everything about all the victims.'

'I understand that, of course, but . . . Well, I just don't like passing on conjectures; there are quite enough malicious gossips as it is.'

'Conjecture?' said her husband, cocking one eyebrow.

'That's all it is.'

'Tell that to my old RSM.'

'Your RSM had an even nastier mind that you have.' She turned back to Alvarez. 'If I tell you something, do you promise not to pass it on?'

'Of course I won't, señora, if it proves to be of no consequence.'

'He's a man who isn't very good at looking after himself; he can't cook or do any of the housework . . . Not that that makes him unique!'

'As I've always said, why keep a dog and bark,' commented Street.

'It's a wonder you didn't say bitch . . . Anyway, ever since we first met him, he's had someone in the house to help for as long as he could afford. When he lived here, that was for just a few hours a week, but when he moved to his flat in Palma it was all day, every day. Initially there he had a gem of a woman, but she was a widow and her son got a job somewhere on the Peninsula and she moved to be with him. After her, there were a succession of women who weren't any good . . .'

'And whom he hadn't the guts to get rid of,' cut in Street. 'Even asked Madge to sack one of 'em.'

'You just don't understand him; won't, more like. He hated sacking her because she'd told him she came from a very poor family and needed his money to save her family from starving. It was all nonsense and I tried to get him to understand, but he wouldn't . . . Anyway, in the end I managed to get rid of her. And then Carolina turned up. She was younger than any of the others had been and she told him she'd been in service with one of the old families in Deya . . . I began to wonder about that when I saw how she did some of the work. The first time we met her she was quiet and respectful and dressed in a maid's apron and if he told her to do something, she did it immediately. But after a while, she stopped wearing an apron and her dresses became very exaggerated.'

'And he looked at her like a cat who's found the cream bowl,' added Street.

Alvarez said: 'Do you know where I can find her? Will she be living in his flat in Palma?'

'I'm sorry, but I've no idea,' she answered.

'She'll be there,' said Street forcefully. 'Making certain that if he pops it she can get her hands on as much as possible.'

CHAPTER 11

It was fact that most cities frightened Alvarez. The size and the press of people and things so reduced his significance as an individual that he could feel himself shrinking and frequently he'd been washed by the fear that any moment he'd disappear altogether. But Palma was different. In Palma, he did not feel at risk. Perhaps it was because much of the city was spacious and attractive, having been designed and built by men who'd understood that there was far more to life than successful commerce. In Palma, he would never disappear.

He drew into one of the parking spaces in the middle of the Paseo Marítimo, switched off the engine, climbed out of the car and locked it. The harbour lay immediately beyond the three eastbound lanes and tied up at one of the outer berths was a very large motor yacht, aggressively streamlined and with twin raked funnels aft. Such a vessel could only belong to an oil billionaire. Looking at the boats in Puerto Llueso or Cala Vescari reminded one that there were still many wealthy people in the world; looking at this ocean-going vessel reminded one that there were a very few so wealthy that money had no meaning outside of power. What was life like when one was rich beyond the dreams of avarice? Was it true that because one could have everything, one could appreciate nothing? In a rare expression of sour grapes, he hoped that it was.

Traffic was heavy and it was several minutes before lights, further along the road, checked the flow of vehicles sufficiently for him to cross to the pavement. He walked past shops, cafés, and a restaurant, to reach the large block of flats in which Leach lived.

At a reception desk in the carpeted entrance hall sat a portly man in uniform. On Alvarez's approach, he lowered the newspaper he'd been reading and with one expert glance determined Alvarez's station in life. He asked, in tones of weary condescension, whom Alvarez wished to see; his tone changed to one of resentment when he learned it was a police matter.

The lift, quick and noiseless, stopped smoothly at the sixth floor and Alvarez stepped out into the carpeted passage. An arrow indicated that Flat 61 was to the right. He turned right and came to a panelled door, made from a dark, beautifully grained wood. He pressed the bell and there was the sound of mellow, expensive chimes. He waited half a minute, sounded the chimes again, waited another half minute and had turned away, satisfied this had been a wasted journey, when the door was opened. The woman in the doorway was in her middle twenties; had she made up less and dressed with more subtlety, she would have been attractive. Her present appearance was not helped by the fact that her hair was mussed up, her lipstick smeared, and the top button of her heavily embroidered blouse was undone.

'Are you Carolina?'

'What d'you want?'

'Cuerpo General de Policía,' he answered, as he stepped inside.

She struggled to overcome her consternation. 'Here, what

d'you think you're doing? This is Señor Leach's place and
he's not here.'

'I know.'

'Then you can't come busting in.'

'I'm investigating the incident in which he was injured
and I need to ask you a few questions.'

'I don't know anything . . .' She stopped at the sharp noise
of the front door banging shut, moved by the slight current of
air caused by the nearby air-conditioning unit.

From one of the rooms, a man shouted, his voice thick with
the slurring accents of Andalucía. 'Hurry up.'

She stared at Alvarez, now scared as well as nervous.

There was another call. 'Are you coming back before I get
chilblains?' The man laughed coarsely.

Alvarez crossed the hall and went down a wide, well lit
passage, off which led several doors; the end one was open.
The bedroom was large and very luxuriously furnished, with
the centrepiece a four-poster bed hung with silk. A man,
naked, very hairy, lay on the bed. 'Jesus!' he exclaimed,
hurriedly pulling a sheet up over himself. 'Are you . . . ?' He
stopped.

'I'm not Señor Leach. He's still in hospital.'

A little of the man's natural cockiness returned. 'Then
suppose you get the hell out of here.'

Alvarez introduced himself as Carolina sidled into the
room.

'I tried to stop him coming through,' she said.

'And didn't succeed. Trust you to screw everything up.'

'Your papers,' said Alvarez.

'Look, I've done nothing . . . except have a bit of fun. And
there's no law against that.'

'Your papers.'

He dragged the sheet free from the foot of the bed so that he
could tie it around his waist in what was a somewhat
ridiculous display of prudery. He crossed the thick pile
carpet to the nearest of three velvet-covered armchairs and

picked up a uniform jacket which had four gold bands on each arm. He brought out a wallet from the inside breast pocket.

'You're a pilot with Iberia?' asked Alvarez.

He tried to show some belligerence. 'That's right, and all they're interested in is me flying the plane safely, not in my private life just so long as that doesn't interfere with the work. So if you just forget what you've seen . . .' He saw from Alvarez's expression that his words were having no effect and angrily brought his identity card out of the wallet and passed it across. As Alvarez examined it, he said bitterly: 'I ought to have known the set-up was crazy. A lovely flat on the front, she said, with more booze that one could drink in a month of Sundays. No one to interrupt us, she said . . . That's a horse's laugh.'

'How was I to know what was going to happen?' she wailed.

'All I can tell you, sister, is that the next time a dame offers me nirvana, I'm going to run like hell in the opposite direction.' He turned and spoke to Alvarez. 'I've done nothing illegal.'

'Have you eaten or drunk anything since you've been in this flat?'

'I swear by all the saints in the calendar that the moment I got in here she dragged me into this room and the last thing either of us was thinking about was eating or drinking.'

'Have you taken anything that was lying about this room?'

'What the hell d'you take me for?'

'Would you like me to tell you, remembering the señor is lying in hospital, injured?'

'But . . . Christ, you know how it goes. In love, it's every man for himself.'

'And no doubt you carry that philosophy into the cockpits of the planes you fly?'

'You've no bloody right to talk like that.'

Alvarez said contemptuously: 'Get dressed and leave.'

'As quickly as I bloody can.'

'But when will I see you again . . .' began Carolina.

'Next century will be too soon.'

She began to cry, because she was scared, because she was being humiliated, and because the situation seemed to demand that she did.

The pilot dressed and left. Alvarez led the way into the sitting-room which was furnished in an overblown, nouveau-riche rococo style, and which had a magnificent view over the harbour and bay. Carolina, who had stopped crying, settled on the settee.

'How long have you known Señor Leach?' asked Alvarez.

'About two years,' she answered in a low, jerky voice.

'Did you know he was married?'

She said sullenly: 'There was a photograph of the wife in his bedroom.'

'Was that his bedroom you were using?'

'What if it was?'

'There wasn't any photograph in sight.'

'He put it away.'

'Or you did?'

'He did, months and months ago.'

'Because you'd moved in?'

'What if I had? Why shouldn't I, if that's what he wanted.'

'But I understand that when he entertained, you had to appear still to be the maid?'

Her mouth drew into bitter lines. 'He won't tell people the truth.'

'Even though you've tried very hard to persuade him?'

'Look, I don't know what you're after, but whatever it is, you're not getting it from me. What he and me did is none of your goddamn business.'

'It's my business to discover whether the boat was blown up because someone was trying to murder Señor Leach.'

'Are you crazy? It was terrorists did that.'

'Perhaps. Perhaps not. Who's Señor Leach's heir?'

It took several seconds for the inference behind the question to become clear to her. When it did, she flinched, as if she'd been struck. 'You don't think . . . You can't.'

'Do you know?'

'No.'

'He was rich?'

'I couldn't kill anyone, however rich.'

'You've found no difficulty in betraying him while he's in hospital.'

'Can't you see the difference?'

'No.'

'Oh my God! It's like talking to someone out of the Ark. Pedro's being here was . . . It was just . . .' She gestured with her hands, trying to make him understand how little significance should be placed in what had happened.

'What kind of a man is the señor?'

'I don't know what you mean.'

'Is he kind?'

'I suppose so.'

'Strong; plenty of macho?'

'You've got to be joking!' Her scorn was immediate. But the moment she'd spoken, she regretted the words. She nibbled her full lower lip.

'Tell me what he is, then.'

She struggled to find words which would not increase his contempt. She hated this detective who mentally was living in the Dark Ages, but she also feared him, instinctively understanding that there was danger for anyone who transgressed his outmoded standards. 'Like I said, he's kind; and always trying to help. Very polite. But he won't . . . He never really stands up for himself.'

'Would you say he's got many enemies?'

'Someone like him doesn't have enemies; people are just scornful of him.'

'As you are scornful of him?'

'That's not what I meant.'

'When you started work here, did you have a novio?'

'I suppose now you're going to read me a lecture?'

'Is he still your novio?'

'No.'

'Because he learned about your relationship with Señor Leach?'

'Men are all the same. They reckon they can enjoy life, but a woman musn't.'

'What's his name?'

'He's nothing to do with you.'

'He might be, if he was very angry when you threw him over for Señor Leach.'

She drew in her breath sharply. 'You're mad to think like that.'

'Mad to think there might still be one man of honour left on the island?' he answered, careless of the irony in his question.

Alvarez slowly climbed up to the third floor and walked along to Suau's office. The room was empty. Gratefully he sat down and relaxed. He looked at his watch. It was already eight o'clock, which meant he couldn't get back home much before nine . . .

Suau rushed into the room and yet despite his hurry he looked as crisply neat as if this were the beginning of the working day and not almost the end. 'There you are at last! Where the devil have you been all day?'

'Señor, you ordered me to question a great number of people . . .'

'I know exactly what I told you to do and I also know that the morning should have been more than enough time in which to do it.' He sat behind the desk. He straightened a file which had been knocked very lightly out of line. 'Well, what have you learned?'

As Alvarez gave a résumé of the interviews, he made notes in his small, precise handwriting. At the conclusion, he said:

'Then it would appear at this stage that if the motive was not terrorism, Leach was unlikely to have been the intended victim?'

'Unless the novio of Carolina tried to gain revenge.'

'No one behaves like that these days.'

People like Suau didn't, thought Alvarez. Suau had his emotions under the strictest control. But someone whose emotions were far more responsive, who had loved deeply but blindly, who had seen his sweetheart stolen by a man whose only asset was his wealth . . .

'What about the local?'

'The local what, señor?'

'The boatman, Rullán, of course. Have you uncovered a possible motive for his murder?'

'Not yet. And since he's an ordinary man, not well off, whose wife left him so that he now lives a very solitary life, what possible motive could there be?'

'Surely your convoluted imagination is capable of supplying at least one labyrinthine suggestion?'

'No, señor.'

'You disappoint me! . . . Then for the moment we need only to consider Señor Todd and Señor Kendall. We now know that Kendall was less than honest in his business and at least one man had cause to hate him and probably threatened him. We also now know that Todd had a number of affairs, often with married women, so that there are a number of cuckolded husbands, any one of whom may have been after revenge . . . Why haven't you any of their names?'

'It's difficult for obvious reasons to discover the identities of the ladies concerned.'

Suau folded his arms across his chest. 'Inspector, it becomes a sign of inefficiency continually to be faced with difficulties.'

'But if there simply hasn't been the time . . .'

'As I have previously mentioned, an efficient detective makes time . . . I thought you had a lead through Señora

Williams. Have you spoken to her on the subject?'

'Not when I've been rushing round the island all day . . .'

'I would hardly describe your action as rushing when I entered this office a moment ago.'

'I'd just got back and was exhausted . . .'

'Exhaustion is purely a state of mind. Go and question her now.'

'As you say, señor.' He paused. 'Only . . .'

'Only what?'

'I do wonder if it might not be better if you questioned her.'

'Why?'

He visualized her blue eyes which changed their shade so rapidly, her sensuous lips, her bronzed, voluptuous body . . . 'She can be a very difficult woman,' he answered, embarrassed by the thought of having to explain what he meant by 'difficult'.

'And you think I might get more out of her?'

'Yes, señor,' he answered, not bothering to dent the other's self-esteem by explaining that in one sense he had been thinking in terms of less, not more.

CHAPTER 12

The baker in Calle Desping cooked lechona so perfectly that the gods on Olympus would have turned aside from their ambrosia to sample it; even Dolores, an egotistical cook if ever there was one, admitted this. And so, when she wanted to give her family a very special treat, she sank her pride and asked the baker to cook it for her.

She had bought the half suckling pig the previous day after much agonizing over which of the six halves for sale at the butcher was the best. In the morning she had laid it out in the special cooking dish and had carried this along to the bakery and handed it to the elder son of the family. When the

morning's bread baking was completed, he had poured over
the joint, and the three others he'd also been asked to cook,
the seasoning mixture which was a family secret—they
would admit that it contained brandy, garlic, thyme, and
marjoram, but would not list any more of its ingredients
—and had left the meat to marinade. Then, in the early
evening, he had put the four dishes into the smaller of the
ovens—last relined thirty-two years before and still wood-
fired—and the meat had cooked slowly and to perfection.

At a quarter to eight, Dolores ordered Jaime to take her to
the bakery. On the drive back, the car was filled with the
smell of the cooked meat and this was so rich and tinglingly
provocative that Jaime decided of his own free will there was
no time for a drink. Unfortunately Alvarez was not back, but
some sacrifices were too great to be considered and the family
ate. The meat that was left was put in the oven to keep warm.

When he arrived home, the lingering smell of the lechona
made him forget to tell everyone how exhausted he was. 'By
God, I'm hungry!'

'It's good,' said Jaime, just before he belched with Arabic
appreciation.

Juan, who'd eaten so much that for once he was not eager
to rush out into the street to play, said: 'If you can't finish
what's left, Uncle, I'll have it for breakfast.'

'You think there's too much for me?'

After a moment, Juan sadly shook his head.

Dolores went into the kitchen, but almost immediately
looked out. 'There was a telephone call for you,' she said
curtly, before disappearing once more.

'Who was it?' he called out. There was no answer. He
looked at Jaime, who shrugged his shoulders, crossed to the
doorway. Dolores was lighting one of the burners on the
stove. 'Who was the call from?'

She blew the match out, put a saucepan on the burner,
turned up the gas.

'Who was the telephone call from?' he asked a second time,

although Dolores's manner had made the answer fairly certain.

She picked up a wooden spoon and stirred the soup. 'It was that foreign woman again.' It sounded as if her whole day had been interrupted by a stream of calls.

'What did she want?'

'It was very difficult to understand her.'

There's none so dense as will not understand, he thought with uncharacteristic lack of charity. 'I'd better ring her back, then.'

'She said she'd be out.'

'Oh!'

Dolores tasted the soup, went to a cupboard and brought out a small pot of garlic salt; she added the smallest possible pinch of this and stirred vigorously.

'Did you gather why she was ringing?'

'She said you'd promised to go and see her and you hadn't.'

'I didn't have the time. Anyway, Comisario Suau said he'd speak to her.'

'He did.' She tasted the soup again, nodded with appreciation.

'Then what's the trouble?'

'She didn't like him or his manner.'

'I hope to God she didn't say anything to his face?'

She shrugged her shoulders.

'And that was all she wanted to tell me?'

'She said you must go and see her tomorrow.' Dolores's tone was now even more critical; only a foreign woman could lack all sense of modesty and dare to speak so openly.

'I will if I've the time . . .'

'And I'm to tell you that if you don't, she'll be very, very annoyed. And now leave me in peace to get on with your meal, will you?' She bent down and briefly opened the oven to make certain the Lechona was being held at the right temperature.

His first, brief thought was that clearly Dolores had understood Zoe very much better than she was prepared to admit. His second, very much deeper thought was to wonder how Zoe would behave if she became very, very annoyed. She was determined, careless of other people's opinions, and shameless. His mind raged over a series of ever more outrageous possibilities. She might even, he concluded with horror, find out what his address was, drive over, and create a scene in front of the neighbours. And then unless he shut her up immediately, they'd treat him with contempt because by letting a woman act like that, he was proving to be less than a man. And Dolores would know bitter shame because what affected him, affected her. But how did one shut up a hunting leopard? . . . He had no option but to go to her house as she demanded.

Juan had finally gone out of the house and Alvarez went over to the chair in which he'd been sitting and settled. Jaime looked at him, frowned, said: 'Is something up?'

He shook his head.

'But you look as if . . . Here, you need this.' He passed over the brandy he had just poured himself.

Alvarez drank.

'Something is the matter, isn't it?' Jaime seldom suffered any tactful reluctance to pry into another's problems.

Alvarez sighed. 'She's forcing me to go and see her.'

'Who is?'

'One of the people I've had to question.'

'But why should that get you all uptight?'

'The thing is, I know she wants me to go to her place because . . .'

'Because what?'

Alvarez looked at Jaime.

'Are you saying she fancies you?'

He nodded.

'What the hell's wrong with that? . . . Or has she got a face worse'n Eloísa's?'

'She'd make a ninety-year-old priest lift his soutane.'

'Then why sit there complaining?'

'I'm scared of losing my soul.'

'I wish to God a hot bit of stuff was after my soul,' said Jaime, angry at Alvarez's stupidity. He went over to the cupboard and poured himself an even larger brandy than the one he'd passed across.

On Sunday the temperature rose still higher. Wells which had not yet dried up were down to historically low levels; where there was no irrigation, the land was parched brown and even the leaves of trees hung limp while the sun beat down on them. In the towns, people crossed roads merely to walk on the shady sides and shops with air-conditioning did an increased trade; on the beaches, holidaymakers sunbathed themselves all shades of red, sometimes to the point of requiring medical attention.

In his 600, Alvarez perspired freely despite the windows and ventilator being fully open. He passed a field in which a man and a woman, both wearing straw hats with very wide brims, were irrigating crops of tomatoes, peppers, beans, and aubergines, and suddenly the sight of their toiling flicked his mind back to a scene from his childhood. He'd been out in a field with his father, who'd been irrigating onions. A neighbour in the next field had shouted something. His father had looked up briefly, then concentrated on using a mattock to lift out a scoop of soil to allow the water, fed from a large estanque, to flow into a fresh channel, and dropping the soil to plug the preceding one. The neighbour had finally come across to them and had spoken excitedly. His father had shown no interest and had continued to work. Eventually, the neighbour had left and even at his age, Alvarez had understood that he had been annoyed by the stolid way in which his exciting news had been received. Over their meal that evening—coarse bread, vegetables, a little homemade cheese—his father had remarked that it seemed war had broken out on the Peninsula. The rest of the family had received the news with the same lack of emotion as he had earlier. The war was far too distant an event to concern them . . . Only it hadn't been and it had reached out to everyone on the island and had turned a hard life into one of poverty, suspicion, fear, and tragedy . . .

The town of Sinyola, just under a kilometre from the quarry, had been built on and around a hill, as this had provided a defence against maurading Moors. The single road leading into it ended at the square in front of the church, three-quarters of the way up the hill. The church, he remembered, possessed a relic of great antiquity and holiness. He sighed. He wished he could believe in relics and their miraculous powers.

There had been no recent building on the approach to the town and the houses were made of sandstone blocks and their exteriors were graceless and bleak, giving no indication of the comfort and rough charm of many of the interiors. He turned right at the first side road, braked to avoid a child who was playing in the middle of the road and, as was quite normal, was totally oblivious to traffic, braked again when a dog ran almost under the front wheel, finally stopped in front of No. 14. There was no pavement and he stepped out of the car and pushed through the bead curtain across the front doorway. Once inside, he called out.

The quarry manager, Montis, entered the room. He shook hands with careful formality. 'Shall we stay here or go through?'

The question was really asking whether this call was going to be more formal than friendly, in which case they would stay, or more friendly than formal, when they'd go through to the everyday living-room. 'Wherever's easiest and causes the least trouble,' Alvarez replied.

They went through and sat. Alvarez said: 'You rang in to say you've two blokes who spoke to a couple of foreigners who seemed interested in the explosives used at the quarry?'

'That's right.' Montis began to pull at the calloused fingers of his left hand, causing each in turn to 'crack'. He stopped when he noticed Alvarez's expression. 'You don't like the noise?'

'Makes me feel sick.'

'The wife can't stand it either. But after all the work I've done with 'em, they're full of rheumatism and this helps a bit. I asked a doctor one day why and he couldn't say.' He smiled sardonically. 'There's a lot that doctors can't say.'

'Not that they'll ever admit that.'

'Would you, if you were earning all that money because people think you do know?'

'Never disillusion the customer!' Alvarez smiled. 'Now, about these two men; are they reliable?'

'The answer's yes and maybe. If Bauzá says something, you know that's right; if Moura does, it all depends.' A boy, about six, ran into the room, glanced shyly at Alvarez, went up to his father and whispered in his ear. Montis listened, patted him as he said: 'I'll be along as soon as I can.' He watched the boy run out. 'I've promised to take him to see his aunt and she always gives him a hundred pesetas so he's in a hurry.'

'He's learned what's important in life, then.'

'They do that soon enough these days . . . About Bauzá and Moura. They agree on what happened, but disagree on one or two of the facts.'

'How well can they describe the two foreigners?'

'You'll have to talk to them to find out. When Bauzá came along after me wanting to know about anyone who'd shown any interest in the explosives, I told him to keep the full story for whoever came to find out about it.'

'Fair enough. Where do they live?'

'Bauzá's two streets up on the right, number seventeen; you can't miss it because the shutters are green. Moura lives in a finca on the Palma road, roughly a kilometre out of the village. You can tell his place by the banana palm; he says

every year he's grown bananas, but if you ask me that's a
load of nonsense—there's never a winter when the wind isn't
cold enough to damage it. But he'll never admit to failure.'

'You didn't see the foreigners?'

'Didn't know about 'em until yesterday when Bauzá spoke
to me.'

Alvarez stood. 'I'd best move on and have a word with
them. Then you can take your son off to see his aunt. I hope
she remembers the hundred pesetas.'

'If she doesn't, he'll very soon remind her.'

Alvarez drove up to the second road on the right and the
house with green shutters. Bauzá could have been any age
between forty and sixty, his leathered skin being contradicted by the brightness of his eyes, his baldness by the easy
way in which he moved.

He led the way through the house to an open patio at the
back which was bounded on two sides by his own house, on
the third side by the house next door, and on the fourth by a
high stone wall. Two orange trees grew in a small bed in the
centre of the square and these bore a number of small, hard
green oranges; along one wall had been trained a vine which
was laden with bunches of unripe grapes. Two canaries hung
high in a cage to escape maurading cats. A couple of chairs
were set out in the shade and they sat on these. From
somewhere quite close came the noise of a radio, volume
turned high, playing pop music.

Initially, Bauzá was nervous and ill at ease, but Alvarez
had the ability to reassure and soon Bauzá was talking freely.

'It was Monday. I know that because my daughter-in-law
was still with us. Me and Carlos was sitting by the side of the
road, having merienda, when we saw 'em, walking; as I said
to him, anyone who walks in this heat when he doesn't have
to is crazy.

'They stopped and asked if they was on the right road to
Laraix. I told 'em, only if they wanted to go the long way

round. So one of 'em took off his pack and brought out a map and I showed him where to go back to and where to turn on to the right road.'

'They spoke to you in Spanish?'

'It was one of 'em did all the talking to us. He was difficult to understand on account of his accent.'

'Did they speak to each other in a foreign language?'

'That's right.'

'Can you say what language it was?'

'Weren't French or English. Can't say no more'n that.'

'What happened after you'd told them how to get to Laraix?'

'The one who spoke a bit of Spanish said he was thirsty and would we like a drink with 'em. He got a bottle of brandy out of his pack.'

'And while you were drinking, he asked you about the quarry?'

'Wanted to know if we worked in it, what kind of rock it was, what the rock was used for, how was it graded. Said his uncle owned a quarry and made a lot of money out of it. As I said to him, the only person to make anything out of our quarry is the owner; I'm bloody sure we don't.'

'And he asked about the explosives that were used?'

'Did we do much blasting, was it still dynamite.'

'How much did you tell him?'

'Everything.' His concern was obvious. 'I didn't see no reason not to. I mean, I couldn't know someone was going to start blowing up a boat.'

'Of course you couldn't. Did he want to know where the explosive was stored?'

For the first time, Bauzá did not answer readily. Alvarez waited, showing no sense of impatience.

'I'll tell it to you straight, I did say it was in the shed, but I don't remember now whether he asked or I just told.'

'Did he ask more detailed questions about the explosive, like how much was usually kept in the shed, what kind of lock was on the door, whether there was a guard at night?'

'No, nothing like that.'

'What happened when you'd all finished talking?'

'They put their packs back on and left.'

'Did they mention where they'd come from that morning?'

'No.'

'But they were definitely heading for Laraix?'

'Asked if the hostal would be full. I told 'em, I wouldn't know.'

'Can you describe them for me?'

Bauzá looked worried. 'I'm no good at that sort of thing.'

'Just do the best you can.'

'They were both a good bit taller than me, and bigger.' He came to a stop.

'What sort of age d'you reckon they were?'

'Twenty-five; something like that.'

'What colour was their hair?'

'Both of 'em was fair.'

'And were they dark-skinned?'

'They were sunburned, but you'd expect that, wouldn't you, with them walking around at this time of the year.'

'Suppose they hadn't been sunburned, d'you think they'd have been dark, like the gipsies, or light-skinned, like the tourists when they first arrive?'

'Don't know as I can really say.'

'How were they dressed?'

'Shirts and shorts. And they were wearing shoes that looked near as strong as the ones we have at work.'

Alvarez watched a humming-bird hawk-moth investigate a flower on a climbing geranium and then dart sideways in a manœuvre that would have shamed a helicopter. 'D'you gain any sort of an idea how long they'd been on the island?'

'They never said nothing about that.'

'Or how much longer they reckoned on staying?'

'Didn't say nothing about that neither.'

That about covered all the questions, Alvarez thought, as

one of the canaries began to sing. It would be very easy and pleasant to drift off to sleep, wafted along by the subtle scent of the two orange trees.

Moura's house consisted of a series of small, boxy structures, each joined on to the side of the preceding one. The reason for so unattractive a style was a practical one. Permission to build a house was difficult to obtain, but an owner was allowed to add to an existing building a proportion of the total floor space as an open patio. Therefore, a man in Moura's position built the permitted extension, waited until any interest in this had totally subsided, then walled in the spaces between the pillars to turn the patio into a room. Since his house was now larger, the next patio he built was permitted to be larger also . . .

They sat on the latest patio, facing a well whose head had been built in stone in traditional shape; a bucket, secured to a chain which ran through a single pulley, rested on the wall. Ten metres beyond the well was a pigsty, built of sandstone blocks, from which came frequent bad-tempered squeals.

'They were Swedes,' said Moura. He was considerably younger than Bauzá and far more aggressive in manner. Many of his statements were made belligerently, as if he constantly expected to be contradicted.

'They mentioned they were from Sweden?'

'I recognized the language they spoke to each other.'

'Then you speak Swedish?'

'I've heard people speak it on the telly, so I know what it sounds like.'

'How would you describe them?'

'They were no taller than me and not so broad-shouldered.'

'Fair-haired?'

'One of 'em was, the other was dark and a bit woolly.'

'Were they dark-skinned?'

'They was both light-skinned.'

'But sunburned?'

'Not particularly.'

When it came to describing them, thought Alvarez, it was as if he and Bauzá were talking about two different pairs of men. 'They were very interested in the quarry?'

'They wanted to know all about it. The one of 'em who spoke Spanish said an uncle of his owned a quarry back in Sweden.'

'He definitely mentioned Sweden?'

'If he's Swedish, that's where his quarry's going to be, isn't it?'

'Were they particularly interested in the explosives?'

'Wouldn't stop talking about 'em.'

'How did the subject first come up?'

'They asked.'

'Just like that?'

'That's right.'

'Did they tell you where they'd walked from?'

'Never said.'

'What about where they were going to?'

'Laraix. Asked if there'd be a room in the hostal. Old Cristian bumbled on about not knowing, but as I told 'em, it's not often full and even if it is, the owner'll squeeze more in; the old sod can't turn down a profit.'

Alvarez asked a few more questions and the answers either confirmed what Bauzá had earlier said or further convinced him that where the evidence conflicted, Bauzá's version was to be preferred, as Montis had suggested.

He returned to his car, but did not immediately drive off. If he went straight to Cala Vescari he'd arrive around lunch-time. There was no certainty that Suau would be aware of that fact. So wouldn't it be better to go on to Laraix and check at the hostal to discover whether the two walkers had arrived and booked in Monday night? Especially since one of the two restaurants at Laraix had a reputation for good cooking.

CHAPTER 13

In 1345, a young virgin had been tending sheep on the side of a hill in the Laraix valley when Mary had appeared and commanded her to build a chapel on the spot on which she then stood. Frightened, she had deserted the sheep and had run back to her crude stone home where she told her mother what had happened. That evening, the elders of the village had gathered together to consider the matter. They were an isolated community, virtually cut off from other villages because it took a mule a day to cross the mountains. They had no priest to advise them and the nearest holy man, a hermit who lived in a cave two kilometres away, invariably became possessed of the devil if approached and asked for help, so it took them a long time to come to the conclusion that although the girl was known to have an unusually vivid imagination, it would be safer to erect a small cairn—not where the girl said she'd been commanded to build the chapel, but on the floor of the valley where the task would be so very much easier. The next morning they'd erected a cairn and two women picked some wild narcissi and laid these by it.

The following morning it was discovered that the cairn had been knocked down and the flowers scattered. The superstitious spoke of divine intervention, but the more practical preferred the explanation that they had not built the cairn as well as they might have done and a cow or a goat had knocked it over. They rebuilt it, with considerable more care. The two women picked twice as many wild narcissi and laid them in two bundles, one on either side, just before dark.

At daybreak there was panic. The cairn had once again been destroyed and the flowers had been shredded before being scattered. The elders of the village came to the only possible conclusion—the girl had had a true vision. So they began to build a simple chapel on the side of the hill. On the day it was completed, the girl was walking across a meadow when her right foot kicked something out of the ground; a small wooden image of the Virgin Mary.

The valley ceased to be isolated, although until the advent of the motor-car it could never be anything but remote; from all parts of the island, and even from the Peninsula, people came to kneel before the image, pleading for divine intercession in their lives. There were many miracles. The simple chapel was knocked down and in its place was built a church of some magnificence. A monastery was added, together with quarters for pilgrims and their beasts. And much later still, after the metalled road had been completed, a memento shop, a post office, a museum filled with the discarded crutches and other silent witnesses of past miracles, and flush lavatories, together with two restaurants, a café, and a hostal, were provided for the tourists.

Alvarez carefully chose a bay in the large car park that was in the shade. He stepped out and stretched—a Seat 600 was not the most comfortable car for the switchback journey over the mountains—then walked along the road and through the main gateway into the grounds and down past the beds filled with gloomy bushes and cacti to the hostal, on the ground floor of which was the café.

Three buses had recently arrived and the tourists, having visited the church and the memento shop, were now in the café, eating and drinking as they waited impatiently to be taken on to the next attraction, unaware that the owner of the café had a standing arrangement with all bus drivers that the buses should not leave on time. It was several minutes before Alvarez could claim the attention of the owner, a small, sharply built man with the roving eyes of someone who was seldom successfully cheated.

'You want to know who were here Monday night?' the owner said. 'I'll check the register.' He went through a door behind the counter, returned with a large clothbound ledger. He opened the ledger and ran his right forefinger down a list of names. 'Monday night, nine people, six of 'em from the night before. The three newcomers were together, two men and one woman from Stuttgart.'

'What about Tuesday night?'

'Six left and four arrived. A married couple from Valencia and two men from Rennes, in France.'

'What sort of age were they?'

He thought back. 'Youngish. Seventeen, eighteen; something like that.'

'Not nearer twenty-five?'

'No way.'

'And everyone's down in that book who should be?'

'There's never been anyone stayed here who hasn't been properly registered.'

'I was only wondering if, when things get really busy . . .'

'Then you can stop wondering. Doesn't make no difference how busy we are; everybody goes down in this book.'

Alvarez left the café and walked to the larger of the two restaurants, which lay just outside the grounds. Several of the tables were free and he chose one by a window, through which there was the dramatic view of the southern half of the valley and the stark, fierce mountains which backed it. A waiter brought a menu and he read through it and tried to decide which of the main dishes to choose, knowing full well that later on he would regret not having tried one of the others instead.

Suau paced up and down the office, each time coming to a smart stop and turning with the snap of a guardsman. It was very tiring to watch. 'It is quite certain that the two foreigners at the quarry said they intended to go to the hostal in Laraix?'

'I don't think there can be any doubt about that,' replied Alvarez.

'How long would the walk have taken?'

'It's only sixteen kilometres by road, but the route is a very tortuous one. Remembering they were young and fit, I'd say from four to five hours.'

'Which should have brought them to the hostal Monday afternoon. D'you believe the hostal proprietor when he says no one else stayed at his place Monday or Tuesday?'

'Yes, I do.'

'Are there any villages with accommodation for the public on the road between Sinyola and Laraix?'

'There isn't a village on that road; it's all in the mountains.'

'Then it looks as if we must accept the fact that they did not walk to Laraix and stay the night there. So either they changed their minds or they were lying. Which?'

'It's impossible to say.'

'It is your job to say.'

Alvarez spoke apologetically. 'But so many things could have happened. Perhaps they walked more quickly than I've allowed and they reached Laraix early on and, having visited the church and so on, decided not to stop there the night —they had time to walk out or they could have hitched a lift; perhaps they lost their way and ended up somewhere else; perhaps they just changed their minds after leaving Sinyola.'

'And perhaps they returned to the quarry, broke into the shed, and stole two sticks of explosive and a detonator.'

There was a silence.

'Well?'

'At the moment, señor, it seems that everything is possible.'

'You have their descriptions?'

'As good as I was able to get.'

'Have them distributed to all sectors of the island. Speak to the airport and find what flights went out on Monday and Tuesday and whether the two men were on one of them.'

'That's going to be rather difficult.'

'With you, everything is difficult.'

'But at this time of year, señor, Palma airport is busier than Madrid. I don't know how many flights there are every twenty-four hours, but it must be dozens and dozens and since we don't know the names of the two men or their destination, we're asking the airport staff virtually to do the impossible.'

'Difficult and impossible is negative thinking. Think positively. The efficient detective always thinks positively . . . What was the woman able to tell you?'

'Which woman is that?'

'Señora Williams.'

'I haven't had a chance to speak to her yet.'

'Then go and speak to her now.'

'You don't think it would be best if we both went . . .'

'I do not,' snapped Suau.

On the short drive to the urbanización, Alvarez attempted to rationalize his feelings towards Zoe. He was scared of her? Why? Because she was possessed of more sexuality than any other woman he had ever met? But wasn't it every man's dream to meet a woman whose passions matched his dreams? Because she appeared to have set her cap at him, rather than vice versa? But wasn't the hunter who let it seem he was hunted, in order to make his hunting the more effective, to be congratulated on his cunning? Because he believed that, as he'd unwisely told Jaime, she was after his soul? Soul connoted a spiritual conflict and no one could suggest at the moment that that was what this was. Because if he allowed his emotions to be overwhelmed, he would lose himself? Dolores had once told him that in matters of the heart he was far too open to hurt and therefore he ought to have the sense to steer clear of them. For him, this could easily develop into a matter of the heart, even though initially the basis was physical . . . Then he wasn't scared of her, he was scared of himself. And since over himself he could exert

full control, it was a fear that should and could be groundless
. . . He felt like a man newly released from a nightmare by
awakening.

When she opened the front door, she was wearing a bright
red safari shirt which just reached down to the tops of her
thighs and it would have been possible for this to be her only
garment. His newly acquired, logical courage deserted him.

'Look who's arrived! Do you come in the guise of the
mountain or Mohammed?'

'Señora?' he stammered.

'Señora,' she mocked. 'Oh man of little memory who
cannot remember that my name is Zoe! Or is this just one
more challenge?'

'I'm not trying to challenge you.'

'Aren't you? Are you sure your delightfully wide-eyed air
of nervous innocence isn't the most subtle challenge of all?
I'm not. So I'm going to find out. Come on in, saith the spider
to the fly.' She took his hand in hers and drew him forward.
As he entered, she seemed momentarily to lose her balance
and she fell lightly against him; but not so lightly that he
failed to feel the swell of her breasts. He felt as if he'd been
running hard.

As she regained her balance, she said: 'It's too hot outside
even for me today, so we'll stay in the sitting-room. It's
Sunday, so we won't be interrupted.' She let go of his hand,
after one quick moment of pressure, when they reached the
centre of the sitting-room which, thanks to a large pedestal
fan and the fact that outside blinds had been unfolded to keep
the sun off the windows, was relatively cool. 'You sit there.
I'm going to use the floor.'

She sat on the floor, resting her back against the settee
and with her knees drawn up. One quick, instinctively
programmed look showed him that she was wearing the
bottom half of a bikini under the safari shirt.

'Have you come to apologize? I warn you, unless you do so
abjectly, I shall be extremely hurt.'

'I've nothing to apologize about.'

'No? After refusing to come here as I asked and instead sending along a little squirt who did nothing but ogle me?'

'Surely that put him higher up in your favour?'

'A touch of acid! The man improves all the time.'

'I've come to ask you some questions.'

'The answers are ready—if the questions are the right ones.'

'You said that Señor Todd was friendly with several women?'

'That is a question which doesn't please me in the slightest.'

'And you also said that many of them were married?'

'He was never a man to stand on ceremony.'

'So the husbands must have been very angry?'

'Those with old-fashioned ideas may have been, I suppose.'

'Will you give me the names?'

'Why should I?'

'Because I want to question the husbands.'

'You think that maybe one of them blew up Deiniol? Obviously you haven't begun to understand what kind of a man he really was.'

'Why do you say that?'

'He was an egotistical, conscienceless, hedonistic bastard, but he wasn't stupid. If he'd ever thought a husband was likely to kick up that rough, he'd quickly have moved on to fresh pastures. And talking about them, let's explore some.'

'Last time, you suggested you knew of at least one husband who was aware that his wife was having an affair with Señor Todd and was very angry about it.'

'I've forgotten.'

'You must tell me his name.'

'Must! Is must a word to be addressed to me? And if I won't? The cat-o'-nine-tails?' Her tone became reflective. 'I've often wondered about the relationship between pain and pleasure. What are your thoughts on that?'

'I prefer not to think about it.'

'A man of an inquiring mind should never limit his thoughts.'

It seemed to him that as she stared at him her eyes not only changed the shade of their blue, they grew larger and became the eyes of a hunting leopard. Fool, he thought despairingly, to have believed he could ever escape her.

'Are your thoughts limited now?'

'Yes,' he lied.

'Then first we'd better drink away your limitations. Last time you were here you had a brandy with lots of ice and no soda. Right?'

He nodded. He knew a sharp, ridiculous pleasure that she should have remembered.

She came to her feet in one lithe, feline movement. 'George always claimed that if you wanted to go to bed to sleep, drink whisky; if you were interested in just going to bed, stick to brandy. D'you agree?'

'I've no idea.'

'Limited experience?' She went over to a mobile cocktail cabinet and poured out two large brandies, added soda to one and ice to both, handed one glass to him and then settled on the floor once more. She raised her glass. 'It's supposed to be very infra dig. to say cheers; so cheers.' She drank. 'It's fortunate that most people are so weak they allow themselves to be ruled by social conventions. If they weren't, the tiny minority wouldn't get pleasure from ignoring them. Do you like ignoring conventions?'

'It depends what they are.'

'What are any of them but middle-class morality? Do you have lots of conventions on this island?'

'We used to.'

'You sound sad because some of them have gone? Surely you're not one of those ghastly people who go around declaiming about how much better everything was in the old days?'

'Yes, I am.'

'And so very proud of the fact! What do you most object to—the changing moral values?'

'Perhaps.'

'They've really only changed for the women, haven't they? But being a traditionalist, no doubt you're convinced there should be one moral code for the male and another for the female. Why? Don't you understand that a woman can feel every bit as sexually enthusiastic as a man? Has no woman ever taught you that?'

He did not dare answer.

'So we have one reactionary who is long on tradition, but short on experience. They say travel broadens the mind. What does experience broaden?'

He shook his head.

'Horizons. And once those are broadened, there's no limit to the possible voyages. Where would you like to voyage to at this moment?'

Needing to do something in the belief—probably ridiculous—that any act which broke the flow of events would begin to ease the tension within himself, he went to drink, only to discover that the glass was now empty. She stood, came over, and took the glass from him to refill it.

She returned, to stand directly in front of his chair. 'Have you thought of an answer yet?'

'No,' he replied hoarsely.

'Are you sure? Or are you just afraid to acknowledge it?'

She leaned over to put the glass down on the small occasional table and then rested her hands on the arms of the chair. The two top buttons of the safari shirt were undone and because she was inclined forward he could be certain that she was not wearing a bikini top. The power of the stalking leopard mesmerized him and his final defence crumbled; now she had only to leap to secure her prey. Bells were ringing, signalling her victory . . .

'Damn the phone,' she said.

He watched her leave the room, then picked up the glass and drank the brandy in several quick swallows.

She returned. 'I'm terribly sorry, but I've just got to rush out. That was an old friend and I haven't seen her for simply ages. She's only just been able to find my telephone number and she's leaving the island very soon. I thought I just couldn't refuse to meet her now. You do understand, don't you?'

He nodded.

'Am I forgiven? Please say I am,' she pleaded. Her eyes were wide and mauve.

He said she was forgiven.

'And you'll come and see me again just as soon as you can?'

As he stood, he said that he would.

'You're the sweetest man I've ever met.'

He walked to the door into the hall, came to a stop as he reached it. 'What is his name?'

'What is whose name?' she said, her voice suddenly sharp.

'The husband you mentioned who knew his wife was having an affair with Señor Todd?'

'Old Andy?' Her voice was once more light and teasing. 'An awful bore with absolutely no idea how a gentleman should behave in difficult circumstances.'

'Andy who?'

'Heyhoe. And I really am in a hurry.'

'If you'll give me his address, I'll leave right away.'

'Don't be like that, Enrique. Honest, I hate having to ask you to leave, but goodness only knows how long it is now since I last saw Belinda.'

'Of course you have to see her,' he said, as convincingly as possible.

'You're absolutely marvellous . . . Andy lives in Ca'n Bastón, in a grotty little place which he will talk about as if it were a palace. I don't know the name, but he's on the telephone. And don't be misled by his wife's little-girl act.

She's not the innocent and helpless little creature she tries to make out. When she flutters those badly mascaraed eyes of hers . . . Promise me you won't desert me for her?'

He wished he were a man of words so that he could assure her that there was not another woman in the world who could make him desert her. He wasn't, so he said: 'I may not even see her.'

'I hope not. Now, I must rush and change into something. See you very soon.'

He let himself out of the house. He knew that he ought to be grateful to Belinda for making that call and interrupting events just before they went completely out of control, but he'd seldom thought of anyone with such sharp dislike.

CHAPTER 14

The army base occupied most of the peninsula, which was shaped like a drop which was about to break off from the viscous liquid from which it had formed. Just under three kilometres long, it was ringed with cliffs, some of them sheer and a hundred metres high. It was doubtful if any of the conscripts appreciated the dramatic beauty among which they lived; of far greater importance to them was the fact that their canteen was a bad joke and the nearest café was four kilometres away and that, despite the government's promise to raise it, their pay was still so low that unless their families sent them money, they could seldom afford to leave the base.

Alvarez drove up to the barrier across the road. One of the two guards, automatic rifle slung over his shoulder, came across. Alvarez gave his name and rank. 'I've spoken to Colonel Noguera and he's expecting me.'

The guard nodded, signalled to his companion who raised the barrier by pushing down on the weighted end. Alvarez drove on. The road wound its tortuous way along the peninsula and there was a succession of breathtaking views, each one framed by the vividly blue sea. A man of peace, he accepted the necessity of a standing army, but without any sense of jingoistic pride in this acceptance; however, his gratitude for their presence here was unreserved. But for them, the beauty would almost certainly have been ruined by the tourist trade.

Near the tip of the peninsula the hills died away and the land became reasonably level and this was where the camp was sited. There were twenty-one houses, all to the same design but a few larger than the rest, a dozen army huts, and a considerable number of store buildings. Beyond the camp, dirt tracks radiated out to the concrete gun emplacements which had been built during the Civil War.

The duty officer showed Alvarez into a room that smelled of leather and grease and on the walls of which hung several photographs of ceremonial parades. He remembered his own military training and how he, along with all the other recruits, had jumped to every command without question and he wondered if to-day they still jumped and didn't question or whether the anti-authority attitude of the outside world had penetrated even this stronghold of tradition?

Cifre came into the room. He was old enough for it to be obvious that he had delayed his service by finishing his studies. He was smartly turned out, even though the battle-dress was a bad fit, and he had the dark complexion and sharp features of gipsy or Moorish ancestry; he was good-looking in a hard, reckless manner.

'Grab a seat,' said Alvarez. He waited while Cifre sat at the small table in the centre of the room. 'D'you smoke?'

'When I can.'

He brought a recently opened pack of cigarettes from his pocket and passed it across. 'Keep 'em.'

Cifre muttered a less than fulsome thanks; the army had taught him to be suspicious of generosity. He lit a cigarette.

'I'm making inquiries concerning a motor-cruiser that was

blown up and in which two Englishmen were killed and an Englishman and a Mallorquin were injured. D'you hear about it?'

'No.'

'It happened last Tuesday.'

'Don't get time to read the paper.' He spoke with tight economy.

'It was on the television as well.'

'Don't get time to watch.'

'The injured Englishman was Señor Leach.'

He looked around for an ashtray, failed to see one, flicked the ash on to the floor and then with the care of someone who had learned that guilt was not the doing of a forbidden act but the being found out of having done it, very carefully ground the ash into the rather threadbare carpet with the sole of his right boot.

'The name doesn't mean anything to you?'

'Why should it?'

'He's a friend of Carolina's.'

For a brief moment his face mirrored several emotions —surprise, bitterness, and hurt—then his expression became blank.

'You'll know him as Cyril.'

'Who said I know him?'

'Carolina.'

'That bitch.'

'You were once her novio.'

Cifre smoked. After a while, he said: 'When did you see her?'

'Yesterday afternoon.'

'Is she still living in his flat?'

'Yes.'

'D'you know what that place cost when he bought it?' His tone became incredulous. 'Thirty million!' He reached down and put the cigarette on the floor beyond the edge of the carpet, used his boot to crush out the lighted end, picked up the stub and dropped it into the pack. 'Thirty million pesetas.'

'He's wealthy.'

Cifre didn't realize it, but when he next spoke his features had softened, leaving him looking a little vulnerable and a lot less sure of himself. 'Me and Carolina came from the same village. She was a bit older than me but that didn't matter and we used to go out together and when it was the village fiesta it was always me who took her to the dance.

'I said we'd need money to get married and so I'd start work with my dad. She said being a carpenter wasn't good enough. Didn't make enough money and wasn't respectable. Respectable!' He spoke the word with contempt and despair. 'So I stayed on at the Institute and did BUP and tried to do COU to get into a university, only I kept failing . . . She went on and on that I'd got to get it or somebody respectable like a bank wouldn't have me . . .' He became silent, lost in memories.

'When did she start working for Señor Leach?'

'Something like a couple of years back. Being near to Palma, a lot of the village women work for the foreigners; them paying much more and not making a fuss about anything. I said to her, I didn't want her doing that sort of work; she wouldn't listen and told me I was taking so long to pass the exam and I hadn't enough money to take her out to the kind of place she wanted to go to. I said, all right, I'd start with my dad and earn and take her out. She wouldn't listen.'

'When did you realize what was going on between her and Señor Leach?'

'When she said . . .' He looked up, surprised by what he'd been saying. 'What's that matter?' he demanded roughly.

'Didn't you have any suspicions?'

He looked as if he was going to refuse to answer, then he suddenly blurted out: 'Of course I bloody didn't.'

'What did you do when you found out?'

'What could I do?' It was a cry of despair. 'She used to buy magazines and read about the lives of the rich and famous and she'd dream of being one of them. Then he offered her that sort of a life and even though she used to laugh at him . . . Know something? That hurt more than anything else. That she could do it with a man she jeered at. Just because he was giving her a bit of the life she'd dreamed about.'

And, thought Alvarez, she'd betrayed Leach, who'd granted her her dreams, just as she'd betrayed Cifre. 'Did you meet him?'

'One day . . .' He stopped.

'One day?'

'I used to go into Palma and walk along the Paseo Marítimo and look up at the flat and think . . . and think bloody stupid. And one day I saw her come out with him. He was twice as old.'

'Did you ever speak to him, trying to make him understand?'

He shook his head. 'He was rich.'

For generations, the rich had behaved as they'd wished simply because they were rich, and the poor had suffered simply because they were poor. And even now that the poor were allowed a sight of justice, they still often behaved as if nothing had changed. 'What did you think of him?'

Cifre didn't answer.

'Ever decide to get at him for what he'd done to you?'

'If I'd had my gun when I saw 'em together . . .' He suddenly realized the danger of what he was saying. He tapped another cigarette out of the pack and lit it.

'Have you finished your basic training?'

'Yes.'

'Learned a bit about explosives?'

'What if I have?'

'Someone used two sticks of dynamite to blow up that boat.'

'I didn't.'

'Where were you last Tuesday?'

He hesitated.

'Well?'

'I did the weekend on duty so I had two days off from Monday. I went home.'

'How did you travel?'

'On my motorbike.'

'Were you home all Tuesday morning?'

'I went out.'

'Where to?'

'Looking for a pal.'

'D'you find him?'

'No.'

'So can you prove you didn't go to Cala Vescari?'

'I didn't,' he said violently.

'And plant two sticks of dynamite, stolen from the quarry at Sinyola, on the *Aphrodite*, timed to explode when Señor Leach was aboard her?'

'How could I know when he was going to be on the boat?'

'Tell me. I'd like to hear.'

'I didn't try to kill the sod.'

'But you're not sorry the attempt was made?'

He was silent.

Alvarez said: 'That's all, then, for the moment, except to give me your identity card. I'll know where to get hold of you if I need you again.'

Because there was no quick way of finding out who Leach's solicitors had been and whether he'd drawn up a Spanish will, Alvarez had sent a request to Madrid and asked for a search to be made in central archives. The answer arrived on Monday morning. Suau, without comment, passed him the Telex message. Leach had made a Spanish will; under this, everything he owned in Spain was left to his wife.

Alvarez said gloomily: 'If he'd left even a proportion of the estate to Carolina, that would have given her a motive; she

could have inveigled Cifre to join her because, despite everything, he still loves her and he hates Leach. And that would
answer the question, how did the murderer know when the
boat was sailing; she must have known. He lives close enough
to Cala Vescari to reach there in a short time on his bike . . .
How can Carolina get her hands on that money now, or at
least some of it, despite the will? Is she planning to challenge
the will? Have our courts begun to follow the American ones
and grant palimony? Or—and this would divert suspicion
—has she found a way to have a direct interest in the money
after Señora Leach inherits it? Perhaps she made contact
with the señora earlier on, without revealing her relationship
with the señor . . .'

'Be quiet,' shouted Suau.

'Señor?' said Alvarez, startled.

'Superior Chief Salas said that you were incapable of handling a case in the way that a normal, sane, responsible,
logical, rational detective would. At the time I considered
that he was exaggerating; but now I know . . .' He paused, to
control his anger. 'Now I know he was guilty of gross
understatement. From the beginning of the case, the facts
have been as clear as the assumption to which they lead. Yet
you have done all you can to introduce extraneous and
irrelevant details, culminating a moment ago in an assess-
ment of what might have been had Leach's mistress been
mentioned in his will—knowing full well that she wasn't!'

'But remembering what London said . . .'

'This morning, other reports came through.' Suau sorted
through the papers on his desk, picked up two. 'There are
two hotels and two hostals within ten kilometres of Sinyola
—all to the south. At none of these did two men, resembling
those who were at the quarry, spend Monday or Tuesday
night.' He dropped one of the sheets of paper on to the desk.
'There is a thrice weekly flight from Palma to Tripoli, used
by men who are working in the Algerian oil industry and
whose families live on this island during their tour of duty.

Last week, two seats had been booked on the Sunday, Tuesday, and Friday flights, in the names of Winqvist and Arendt. Businessmen often make repeat bookings when they don't know on which flight they'll actually be travelling. These two seats were used on the Tuesday.'

'Are you, señor, assuming that they were the two who spoke to the quarrymen?'

'To a straightforward mind, it seems very possible.'

'But . . . but we've nothing to say they weren't what they made themselves out to be. I don't see that the fact that they didn't sleep at the Laraix hostal is necessarily of any real significance. They could have decided not to stay the night there; they could have walked faster than we've allowed for . . .'

'We've been through all this before.'

'I was only . . .'

'Alvarez, tell me one thing. Do you ever admit to being wrong?'

'Frequently, señor. But in this case I have a feeling . . .'

'I see. The entire world is watching us, judging us, ready to criticize every aspect of our handling of the case, but rather than prove we are carrying out our investigations according to the evidence, you would have everyone know that we are guided by your feelings?'

'It's so difficult to explain,' said Alvarez hopelessly.

'Somewhat naturally.'

'But there is still the original query raised by London . . .'

'There was, but that has been fully covered . . . It is my intention to report to the superior chief that although it has, as yet, proved impossible to obtain conclusive proof, there is virtually no doubt that these murders were an act of terrorism.'

'I suppose if we say that, then in the light of what's happened in other countries we can't really be blamed for failing to arrest the terrorists.'

'Such a consideration has no room in my decision.'

'No, of course not.' Alvarez hesitated, then said: 'But I can't forget that report from London.'

'Which was equivocal.'

'I suppose so . . . There is just one other point. I haven't interviewed Señor Heyhoe yet.'

'Who's he?'

'The husband of one of the women with whom Señor Todd probably had an affair. I rather think he did, in fact, threaten to kill Señor Todd.'

Suau drummed on the desk with his fingers.

'I'm sure it would be best, señor, if we can show that we've left no stone unturned.'

'With you around, that means uprooting a whole bloody beach.'

CHAPTER 15

The urbanización called Ca'n Bastón was eight kilometres inland, situated in part of what was, for the island, an extensive pine wood. In advertisements in the United Kingdom, Western Germany, and Scandinavia, copywriters spoke enthusiastically of sylvan glades, morning birdsong, and vistas of timeless beauty. There were glades, but these were usually unapproachable because of brambles and other thorned weeds; such birds as escaped being slaughtered by gun or trap did sing, but only very quietly, knowing that Mallorquins were contemptuous of closed shooting seasons; and the vistas were only visible six hundred metres beyond the western limit of the urbanización, due to a fold in the hill which backed the area.

The Heyhoes' house was one of several bordering a side road, all of which had been built for economy budgets. In the sunlight of high summer, they were dully unattractive, while in the gloom of an overcast winter's day they looked like the setting for one of Ibsen's less jolly plays.

The Heyhoes were much as Zoe had suggested. He was pompous, pedantic, and aggressively uncertain of himself. She was small and petite and had the large, doe-soft eyes which enraptured men who liked doe-soft eyes. She also had a natural taste in clothes and never let her husband's impecunious financial state stand in the way of dressing well.

At first, Heyhoe's manner was both supercilious and condescending, but it changed to an attempt to propitiate when Alvarez made clear the reason for his visit. Penelope's manner remained pleasant, but the expression in her doe-soft eyes suggested a certain thoughtfulness. 'I'd better leave you,' she said, as she stood up.

'You've got to remain . . .' Heyhoe began.

'You know I never stay for men's talk.'

'But this is about . . .'

'I'd rather not hear what it's about, my sweet. I know men do discuss all sorts of things, but I'd rather not have to listen to them.'

'For God's sake, he's come to talk about Deiniol, not tell dirty stories.'

She faced Alvarez. 'You do understand, don't you, Inspector?' She left the small patio, protected overhead by bamboo mats which had been secured to wires, and went indoors.

'I think the señora was a friend of Señor Todd's?' said Alvarez.

'We both were,' replied Heyhoe quickly and with too much emphasis. 'That is, we used to see quite a bit of him when he was over here.'

'Perhaps she was more friendly than you?'

'Who the hell says that?'

'Did you ever threaten Señor Todd because of her friendship for him?'

'Bloody nonsense. As I've always maintained, this is the

worst place on earth for scandal. Trouble is, there's a whole lot of people with no sort of background and nothing to do. As my uncle always said, you can't hide a lack of breeding in horses, dogs, or humans.'

'Señor, did your wife have an affair with Señor Todd?'

He said, trying to instil some authority into his voice: 'You've no right to say a disgusting thing like that. Of course she didn't. Who suggested the filthy lie? Just tell me that —who?'

'I'm sorry, but I have to keep names confidential.'

'It's someone who obviously hated Penny . . . I'll bet I know who it was. That bitch, Zoe Williams. D'you know why she told you that? Because Deiniol chucked her on one side when he . . . Well, when he became friends with Penny; with us.'

'You are saying that Señora Williams was jealous?' Alvarez was aware that his voice had hardened. He longed to ram the lie down the man's throat. Zoe might be many women, but she was not a cheaply vindictive one; of that he was certain.

'You can say that again.'

'So she obviously believed she had cause to be jealous?'

'She . . . All that was happening was that Deiniol had got fed up with her and was taking a bit of notice of Penny and because Zoe had thrown herself at him, she got the wrong idea.'

'But if she got the wrong idea, perhaps you did as well?'

'I trust my wife implicitly.'

'Then why did you say you'd kill him?'

'That's bloody nonsense.'

'I think it is the truth. Señor Todd had a bad reputation with women, didn't he?'

'Yes, but . . .' He stopped.

'So you surely cannot have welcomed his friendship with your wife?'

'I tell you, I trusted her. Why can't you understand that?'

'I understand that you said you were going to kill Señor Todd.'

'No,' he said violently.

'There are witnesses.'

His expression abruptly became one of defeat. He fidgeted with his lips and kept looking quickly at Alvarez. 'Perhaps I . . . A chap can say something which sounds quite different when it's repeated another time.'

'It seems difficult for it to mean anything except you were threatening to kill him because you believed that he and your wife were having an affair.'

'I didn't believe it. But he was putting her in an impossible situation when all the vicious tongues would wag . . . Christ, I need a drink.' He stood. 'What d'you want?'

Alvarez said he'd like a brandy. Heyhoe went into the house. Seconds later, the low buzz of conversation reached Alvarez. He guessed that Heyhoe was trying to get his wife to come out on to the patio to support him and she was refusing because she had a delicate character.

Heyhoe returned with two glasses, a chromium-plated ice container, and a soda siphon, on a tray. He put one glass, the ice container, and the siphon, in front of Alvarez. 'Help yourself, old man. As I always say, if you help yourself, you get what you want, not what someone else reckons you ought to have. I always remember a man in the office who used to . . .'

Alvarez interrupted what threatened to be a long, rambling story, told soley to delay further questions. 'What was the relationship between your wife and Señor Todd?'

Heyhoe drank eagerly. He put the glass down. 'You must understand something. At first, Penny didn't know what he was after. She thought he was just being friendly. She's a good-looking gal and more than one man's taken a shine to her. Deiniol was introduced at a party just after we came out here and he seemed friendly and I've got to admit, we were both a little flattered. There's something about meeting a person who's famous and always on the box . . . Anyway, we went to his place once or twice and he asked us out on his yacht. But after a bit it seemed to me he was trying to . . . Well, I did get a bit worried, but Penny just laughed at me and said I was being silly and famous people always acted like that. So I tried to stop bothering. You see, I knew she'd never ever let me down. And then I had to go back to England for a fortnight and while I was away he asked her out for a trip and she thought other people would be going, so she went. But she was the only other person on the boat and . . . She was forced to make it clear she wasn't like the other women he'd known. He respected her for that. She told me that he said so. When I heard what had happened, I swore she mustn't have anything more to do with him. She told me I was being silly because everything was all right now. We had a bit of a row about it, as a matter of fact; don't usually have rows. In the end, she agreed to do as I said. And then she started going out on her own and when I'd ask her where she'd been, she'd say with Emily. She knew I couldn't stand that stuck-up bitch and so I'd never get talking to her. But one day I was chatting to some people with malicious tongues and they started saying they'd seen Penny out on Deiniol's boat the day before and how understanding of me it was to allow her . . .'

'Is that when you threatened to kill him?'

'I only said that because I was so angry with them and all their beastly insinuations . . . I swear I didn't mean it.'

'But you couldn't any longer be in doubt regarding the relationship between your wife and Señor Todd?'

'If you're trying to make out she . . . All right, she had been out with him once or twice, but only because he amused her. And she'd not told me because she didn't want me to get all upset when there was no need to be. She promised me nothing happened and I believe her absolutely.'

How difficult was it to make himself believe that? wondered Alvarez. He stared at the other houses in sight and wondered how many of the people who lived in them also led twisted lives in which lies were often so much kinder than the truth? 'Señor, where were you last Tuesday?'

'Here.'

'Did you not go out all day?'

'I don't really remember; I mean, one day's very much like another.'

'This day wasn't exactly like any other; two men were murdered.'

'What I was meaning was, time doesn't mean much here. There's no office to go to and not speaking Spanish, we don't have television . . . I just can't remember last Tuesday.'

'Perhaps your wife will be able to?'

'No, she won't.'

'I would like to ask her.'

'I'm sorry, but when I went in she told me she's got a bad headache. And now she's lying down. I don't think it's right to disturb her.'

'You say you can't remember Tuesday. Then you may have gone out in your car, mayn't you?'

'I . . . I suppose so.'

'And you might have driven over to Cala Vescari?'

'No. Definitely not.'

'But if you can't remember?'

'You're confusing me.' He picked up his glass, but found it to be empty. 'What I'm trying to say is, I don't know exactly what I was doing, but I can be certain I didn't go to Cala Vescari because I haven't been there since Penny and I both went together to see Deiniol.'

'Have you ever handled explosives?'

'Why should I have?'

'You might have been in the army?'

'Do I look that thick?' He tried to laugh, but stopped when he realized he was merely sounding foolish.

Alvarez finished his drink. 'There's one more thing. May I have your residencia, please.'

'Why d'you want that?'

'To have the photograph copied.'

'But I swear . . .' He tailed off into silence. He slowly stood, went into the house. When he returned, he handed Alvarez a two-year residencia.

'Thank you,' said Alvarez, as he pocketed it.

'You do understand what I've told you?'

'I have listened very carefully to everything, señor.' Understand the lives they led? Not in a thousand years.

The drive up to the high plateau was for Alvarez a journey which took him out of the mire of greed and lust to the clean simplicity of true values. On the plateau, man had learned that material success was nothing, what mattered in life was to live honestly and never wittingly hurt another.

He stopped the car beyond the blasted oak and climbed out. The dog, curled tail wagging furiously, appeared and started barking at him; a hoopoe, seen as a brief, undulating flash of barred colour, twisted round a tree to vanish; chickens scratched among the litter of leaves; a kestrel hovered overhead; a pig squealed . . . He breathed deeply, revelling in the smell of growth and decay. The man who worked the land came as close to understanding the mystery of life as anyone.

Rullán came out of the house, his heavily lined, weathered face expressing no emotion, not even surprise.

'It's like another world up here,' said Alvarez enthusiastically. 'What wouldn't I give to live in it!'

'No one's stopping you moving,' replied Rullán drily. He shouted to the dog to shut up barking, then led the way round the house to the patio. Without asking, he brought a bottle of wine and two glasses out of the house and set them on the table. Alvarez filled a glass and drank deeply.

He put the glass down and brought out of his pocket the photographs of Cifre, Heyhoe, and Sutherland, taken from residencias or identity card. He passed them over. 'Look through these and say if you saw one of 'em on or around the quay last Tuesday.'

'I told you, I was too busy to see who was on the quay.'

'But you'll have looked ashore from time to time, however busy you were; you must have noticed one or two people.'

'Must I?' Rullán studied the photographs, squinting because of the brightness and because he needed glasses. 'Never saw none of 'em.'

'What about on the Sunday or Monday?'

'No.'

'D'you recognize any of 'em?'

He picked out one photograph. 'He's sailed on the boat. And so's his wife.'

As expected, the photograph was of Heyhoe. 'She's been on the boat more often than he has, hasn't she?'

'What if she has?'

'And that didn't please the husband.'

'That's his business, not mine.'

'Did you ever hear him going at Señor Todd because of her?'

'Him? He hasn't got that much in him; no balls.'

Alvarez took the photographs back. He'd known that in the circumstances the odds had been against Rullán identifying Cifre, Heyhoe, or Sutherland, but he'd still been hoping . . . 'There are two men you could have seen near the boat.' He described the two who'd spoken to Bauzá and Moura at the quarry.

Rullán shrugged his shoulders. 'At this time of the year, with the tourists flooding everywhere, the port's full of men like you've described.'

'They'd have been particularly interested in the *Aphrodite* and there's the possibility they were Swedish.'

'If they were Eskimos, it'd make no difference.'

'Why not?'

'Look, just what the hell d'you think I do when I'm on the boat?'

'Tell me.'

'Cleaning, polishing, checking, oiling, greasing. You never finish on a boat; or if you do, you're no bloody seaman.'

'And what about when you're at sea?'

'Then you work harder.'

Alvarez drained his glass. 'I've been listening to someone who says that Señor Todd liked the women.'

'What if he did?'

'He was worse than a dog chasing a bitch on heat.'

'If they were bitches, what d'you expect?'

'He must have got a lot of husbands angry?'

'You're a great man for the musts. From what I've seen of 'em, the husbands didn't give a damn.'

'Then apart from Heyhoe, you can't name any husband who definitely had it in for the señor?'

'I didn't name him. What I said was, he didn't have the guts to do anything.'

They became silent. Perhaps Suau was right, Alvarez thought. Perhaps he was making a pig-headed fool of himself by refusing to accept the obvious. What if the terrorist group had not immediately claimed responsibility for the explosion? They might so easily have had a security reason for the delay. What if Cifre, Heyhoe, and Sutherland, each did have a strong motive for murdering one of the men on the *Aphrodite*? The gap between wishing a man dead and going out and killing him was an enormous one . . . And yet he had the feeling that he was right and this had not been an act of terrorism; that he could prove it hadn't been if only he were clever and had the wit to see some vital piece of evidence which even now was staring him in the face. But he wasn't clever and he didn't have much wit.

His glass was empty. He reached across for the bottle.

CHAPTER 16

As he drove towards the urbanización, he carefully made it clear to himself why he was going to see Zoe. She had told him about the Heyhoes and had suggested that there had been other husbands who'd had cause to hate Todd. One of them might be of a much stronger character than Heyhoe; strong enough not to have threatened and then weakly hid his mind from the facts, but to have said nothing and have acted. He wanted to know the name, or names. He definitely was not seeing her again because the memory of the way her safari shirt had fallen forward as she leaned over him was tantalizing and torturing his imagination . . .

He parked the car, walked up to the front door of Ca'n Orpoto, and rang the bell. He suffered the now familiar, painful tension. He pictured her, walking towards the door, wearing a bikini that revealed by hiding . . .

The door was opened by a dumpy middle-aged woman who wore a lilac-coloured apron over a long frock.

'The señora's not here,' she said, in answer to his query.

'Do you know what time she'll be back?'

She shrugged her shoulders. 'Maybe tomorrow, maybe next month.'

'Are you saying she's gone away?'

'Yes,' she answered, surprised he was so dense.

'But where's she gone to?'

'How would I know?'

'Didn't she tell you?'

'Her? She does what she liked and never tells anyone.'

'Is she still on the island?'

'I tell you, I don't know nothing except she's not here.'

'Didn't she leave me a message?'

'There's none around I've seen.'

Zoe's last remark the previous day had implied that she'd see him again the moment Belinda had left the island . . . Perhaps there was a message from her at the station which no one had yet bothered to deliver to the third floor . . . He thanked the maid, left.

He parked outside the station and hurried in. The duty sergeant stopped reading the paper long enough to say there'd been no message for him. He went up to the third floor. Suau was not in the office. He searched through the papers on the desk, but there was no message. Yet it was inconceivable that Zoe could have gone away and not . . . And suddenly he realized that the maid had said that Zoe might as easily have gone for a day as a month, but he had imagined the worst and had panicked. But the fact that there was no message made it obvious that she'd only gone for a day; two at the most . . . He brought out a handkerchief and mopped the sweat from his face and neck. There was no fool like an old fool.

Alvarez knocked on the door of Room No. 324 at the clínica and entered. Leach, wearing a lightweight cotton dressing-gown over pyjamas, was seated in the armchair near the window.

'You're looking much better, señor,' Alvarez said.

'My chest still hurts like hell,' replied Leach petulantly.

'I am sorry. What do the doctors say?'

'There's only one who speaks any English at all and then it's so bad that half the time I just can't understand him.'

'Perhaps I can find out something later on . . . But now I hope that you'll help me to find out something.' He walked past the chair to the settee and sat.

'What's the trouble now?' Leach shut the book he'd been reading and put it down on the small table by his side.

'Perhaps you will look at some photographs?' Alvarez produced the photographs and passed them across.

Leach looked through them quickly.

'Do you recognize any of the people?'

'One of them seems to be vaguely familiar, but I'm no good on faces. People get very annoyed when I don't recognize them, but it's not my fault if I've a bad memory.'

'Did you notice any of these men near the boat on Tuesday?'

'I didn't, but I wouldn't have noticed anyone. I was late and Deiniol always made such a fuss about time so I was hurrying all I could . . . Who are they?'

'Just before I explain, have you ever seen two men who look like this?' He described the two men to whom Bauzá and Moura had spoken.

'No,' said Leach impatiently. He fingered the photographs, studied them again. 'I'm pretty certain now I've seen one of 'em somewhere.'

'That will almost certainly be Cifre; Agapito Cifre.'

'Agapito? That's a funny sort of a name.'

'He was Carolina's novio.'

'You mean, he's the man she was going round with before . . .'

'Before she started to work for you and finally moved in.'

'I . . . I know what you're thinking.'

'That shouldn't be too difficult.'

'But it's not like that at all. She and I are . . . We're just good friends.' He spoke as if unaware that his words were one of the most overworked of clichés. 'I don't care what people say.'

'What are people saying?'

He moved very carefully, but still flinched as pain clawed its way up his chest. 'People out here are so malicious. There's absolutely nothing going on between her and me.'

'Agapito thinks differently.'

'What's that matter?'

'That all depends. Some employers would be concerned that their employee's novio had gained a totally false understanding of the situation.'

'I can't help the way he thinks.'

'Not when a word or two from you would set his mind at rest?'

'Would it?'

'He's still very fond of her.'

'That's his affair.'

'You can't see why you should be concerned?'

'No.'

'We are a proud people.'

'All right, so you're proud.'

'We are also old-fashioned; we still recognize honour and dishonour.'

'I can't understand why you're going on like this.'

'Of course you can't,' said Alvarez scornfully. 'Such words no longer have any meaning for you. But what makes you think you can come and live in our country and behave so ignorantly and yet escape the consequences?'

'Escape what consequences?'

'We have a saying: when a man sows weeds, he doesn't reap corn . . . When you forced Carolina away from Cifre, you dishonoured him.'

'I forced her? Are you crazy? If you really want to know, she couldn't run fast enough.'

'You used your money to blind her to her dishonour.'

'I thought you were a detective, not a hail-Jesus man.'

'Being old-fashioned, proud people, we still need to avenge the stains of dishonour.'

It took several seconds for Leach to understand the full meaning of what had been said. His expression became scared. 'Here, are you saying . . . He was trying to kill me, just because of her?'

'I don't know, which is why I'm trying to find out. But until you tell me all the truth, I cannot.'

'But she said . . .' He stopped.

'What did she say?'

'He was just a boy she'd always known and there was

nothing more to it than that.'

'When did she say that?'

'After I told her he'd stopped me in the street one day.'

'Where?'

'Near my flat.'

'What did he want?'

'He went on and on in Spanish, shouting twenty to the dozen, and I couldn't understand a word.'

'But you could guess why he was so upset?'

'I didn't think . . .'

'No, you didn't think. Because you had only contempt for him; for you, he was just a 'native', an inferior who had to put up with the consequences of whatever you chose to do, however you chose to behave.'

'Hey! I've never thought like that.'

'You've acted like that.'

'I tell you, she came running.'

'Seduced by your wealth.'

'Christ! you won't understand.'

'I cannot understand a man who is so contemptuous of the feelings of others.'

Leach flushed. Then his fear overcame his sense of shame. 'It's him who planted the bomb on the boat, isn't it?'

'I've told you, I don't yet know.'

'Trying to get his own back on me. Then you've got to arrest him.'

'I have no proof of his guilt.'

'But you know it must have been him.'

'He denies having any hand in the explosion.'

'Of course he does; you must be a bloody fool if you think he wouldn't. If you won't arrest him, I'll call the consul.'

'You'll find he has no power to intervene.'

'He can't help me?' Leach looked almost as bewildered as frightened. 'Then you've got to do something.'

'Because you're reaping weeds, not corn?'

'Why d'you go on like that? Oh God, I wish I'd never met

her. He'll try again and next time . . . You've got to do something.'

'Have you seen him since he stopped you outside your flat?'

Leach plucked at the tassel on the waist-cord of his dressing-gown. 'Yes,' he said hoarsely.

'When was this?'

'On Tuesday. I saw him on the quayside, just before I went aboard the *Aphrodite*.'

'You are quite certain of this?'

'I'm positive.'

'Why haven't you mentioned it before?'

'I didn't like to cause trouble when I wasn't certain he was trying to murder me . . . That's proof enough to arrest him, isn't it?'

'No.'

'Why the hell not?'

'It's your word against his. He says he was nowhere near Cala Vescari on Tuesday morning.'

'Isn't it obvious he's lying to save himself?'

'No more obvious than that you may be lying to save yourself from what you fear, by falsely implicating him.'

'You've got to believe me, not him.'

'Because he's only a native?' asked Alvarez bitterly. He replaced the photographs in the envelope.

'What are you going to do?' Leach demanded desperately.

'There's little I can do, when you go on lying.'

'But he'll try again to kill me.'

As Alvarez stood, he remembered that Leach had been described as a nothing-man. That was wrong. He was a coward, ready to sacrifice anyone to save himself. By comparison, a nothing-man was someone.

Alvarez stared at the television screen, but had no idea what he was watching. Cifre had said that he'd never spoken to Leach; although Leach had surely lied about seeing Cifre on the quayside on Tuesday, Alvarez was certain that the meeting in the street had taken place. Then how significant was Cifre's lie? Was it the instinctive lie of a man who had panicked when he realized that to acknowledge any actual meeting would be to point the finger of suspicion more directly at himself? Or was it the lie of a man who had calculated that it was safer to risk a lie which might just be found out rather than to admit to a meeting which must suggest that his emotions had been far more openly and strongly involved than he'd been prepared to admit . . .

'Enrique, what's the matter?' demanded Dolores.

He started.

'Are you all right?'

'I'm fine. Why d'you ask?'

'You keep staring at the television screen, but Jaime's switched it off.'

For the first time, he realized that the screen was blank. 'I was just thinking.'

'About her?' asked Jaime, who kept visualizing the woman who was after Alvarez's soul and in consequence had built up a mental picture of such a libidinous character that he was suffering from severe jealousy.

'What's that?' snapped Dolores, her tone now sharp rather than worried.

Alvarez said angrily: 'If you must know, I was thinking about the case.'

Dolores was not so naive as to be diverted that easily. 'I suppose it's the foreign woman who speaks to me as if I were a piece of dirt?'

'She doesn't do anything of the sort . . .'

'And how would you know, when it's me who has to speak to her?'

'She's not that kind of person.'

'I can judge exactly what kind of person she is when she orders me, not asks me, to bring you to the phone.'

Dolores's world was moulded by her, not she by the world.

If it suited her to remember Zoe as imperious, then that was how Zoe had behaved. Recognizing this, Alvarez didn't argue any further, but tried to placate her. 'Foreigners do some things in a different way from us.'

'But not everything,' snickered Jaime.

She stood. 'I am tired; very tired because I have spent the whole day slaving for two men who thank me by treating me with vulgarity and calling me a liar.' She swept out of the room. Such was her air of dignity and occasion that she might have been wearing a ballroom gown and a tiara.

The telephone rang at five forty-five the next morning. Dolores, conditioned to sleep lightly because of the children, awoke immediately. She stared at the window and saw it was only just outlined and so judged the time still to be very early. The ringing continued and she experienced a sharply growing uneasiness; only bad news could possibly be so urgent at such an hour. She prodded Jaime.

'What's matter?' he mumbled.

'The telephone's ringing.'

'Then answer the bloody thing.'

She told him to find out what catastrophe had overtaken them in terms he could not ignore and, loudly cursing the unknown caller, he put on slippers and went downstairs. The call proved to be for Alvarez. Swearing even harder, he returned upstairs, switched on the overhead light in Alvarez's bedroom, and shook his shoulders. 'Someone called Suau wants you. Tell the stupid bugger to telephone at a reasonable hour next time.' He returned to his own bedroom, kicked off his slippers, collapsed back on to the bed, and pulled the sheet over himself. 'Switch the light off, can't you, and let's get some sleep.'

'Why d'you call Enrique?'

'Why d'you bloody think?'

'The call was for him?'

'Of course it was.'

'It was that woman?'

'It was someone from the police. Now, for God's sake, shut up and sleep.'

She switched off the light. Obviously there was some sort of crisis, but it was external to the family and therefore didn't concern or worry her.

Down below, Alvarez replaced the receiver. A Mercedes, driven by Leach, had skidded off a feed road to the motorway, broken through the concrete wall of a bridge, and fallen down on to the motorway below. He had been killed instantly. The traffic police report named it an accident, but in the circumstances there was the obvious probability that it had been murder.

CHAPTER 17

In the clear, absolutely still early morning air, as sparkling fresh as spring, the mountains seemed much closer than they would later on when the sun was up; on Puig Major, the twin domes of the early warning system looked small and insignificant and not grim harbingers of the approach of the four horsemen.

The Mercedes 280 had landed upside down and despite all the built-in strength of the roof the force of the crash had reduced the height of the car by half. Red cones had been placed round it, reducing the eastbound carriage to one lane. Initially, an attempt had been made to extract the body, but the car was so severely compressed that this had soon been given up and now the police were waiting for the mobile crane which had been called out, but had not yet arrived, so that the wreck could be loaded on a lorry.

A traffic policeman came up to where Alvarez stood. 'We've measured the marks and the best estimate is that the car was doing around a hundred and forty k.p.h.'

'Any signs of another vehicle being involved?'

'None at all.'

'So it probably wasn't a direct collision?'

'At that sort of speed, there'd be skid marks of the other car.'

'And nothing to suggest why the Mercedes skidded?'

'Nothing, other than the bend back there.' The policeman pointed up. 'You need to be a smart driver to take that at a hundred and forty. If you ask me, he was just going too fast and lost control. It happens all the time. They think they're Lauda, but discover they aren't.'

He'd still been suffering from his injuries; the need for a sudden and unexpected movement of the arms could easily have caused sharp, crippling pain in the chest. Alvarez looked up at the shattered parapet of the bridge. 'The experts are going to have to go over the car with a fine-tooth comb looking for something that was fixed to break.'

'The only thing left to do with that wreck is dump it.'

'It could have been sabotaged.'

'Yeah?' The patrolman scratched the back of his neck. 'I'll tell you one thing. It'll take a damned good man to say what bust before the crash rather than after.'

Alvarez crossed the hard shoulder and scrambled up the grass bank to the road above and his parked car. He sat behind the wheel, but did not start the engine. The road he was now on led only to the motorway which in this direction served only the airport. So Leach must have been making for there. The speed at which he'd been driving, especially remembering those injuries, suggested panic. Panic because the murderers had shown their hand and he was trying to escape them, never realizing that his car had been chosen as the vehicle of his death? . . . What could he have known that was so dangerous to know?

On the ground floor of the clínica there was a café and beyond that a restaurant; the main entrance was visible from

most of the tables in the café and Alvarez, very aware that he
had been up since the early hours, decided that not even
Suau, who was to meet him here in ten minutes' time, could
reasonably object to his having a quick breakfast. He went
through to the café and at the counter ordered a coffee and an
ensaimada. He had just sat and was about to take his first
mouthful of the ensaimada when Suau entered, looked across
into the café and saw him, and came through. Alvarez
put the ensaimada down on the plate. Despite his earlier
optimism, he braced himself for a short, sharp lecture on
slackness.

Suau moved out one of the free chairs and sat. ''Morning.'

Alvarez could not hide his astonishment at such a display
of friendliness.

'I wouldn't say no to a coffee and an ensaimada.'

'I'll get them for you, señor.'

As he stood at the counter, waiting for the hissing espresso
machine to complete its work, he wondered if Suau were not
feeling too good? At least he wouldn't have far to go for
treatment.

Back at the table, Suau tore off the top of an individual
sugar pack and emptied the contents into the cup. He stirred
for several seconds, his mind plainly not on what he was
doing. Then, as he withdrew the spoon, he cleared his throat.
'Alvarez, it's quite clear that we must accept the possibility
that this crash was not an accident, but was deliberately
engineered.'

'Yes, señor.'

He bit off a mouthful of ensaimada and ate it. When he
swallowed, his rather prominent Adam's apple surged up
and down. 'If he was murdered, then it must be directly
connected with the previous murders.'

'Yes, señor.'

'In which case, those first two murders were not the work
of terrorists.' He drank some coffee. 'Last night, I telephoned
the superior chief . . .' There was a strange note in his voice;

in a lesser man it might have been described as peevish resentment. 'I told him that, because of all the known evidence, it seemed probable the explosion was the work of terrorists, that the two men seen near the quarry might well have been those terrorists, and that these two were using the identities of Winqvist and Arendt when they flew off the island on Tuesday evening . . . But at no time did I say that any of these statements was established fact; I could never have gone that far when so much is still conjecture and we have not yet heard from the Algerian police whether two men with those names can be identified as working in the oil fields . . . You will, of course, bear me out that at no time have I been so specific?'

Alvarez, uncertain where all this was leading to, said carefully: 'It's a bit difficult for me to say anything like that when I wasn't around when you spoke to the superior chief . . .'

'Good God, man, you know as well as I how I've viewed the evidence all along.'

'Yes, señor, I do.'

'And we are a team, are we not?'

'I suppose one could say that . . .'

'I do say it. I also say that the members of a team play together.' Suau tore off a piece of ensaimada and began to roll it between thumb and forefinger. 'Before coming here, I telephoned the superior chief to inform him of the death of Leach. Naturally, I pointed out that at this stage the car accident inevitably casts doubts on the theory that the explosion on the boat was the work of terrorists. Regrettably, the superior chief said . . . He referred to me in terms which no man should ever employ when describing someone in his team. It is not my habit to criticize a superior officer, but I am bound to say that his language was emotionally coloured and totally unwarranted.'

'Why should he be so upset? After all, this merely confirms what I've been saying from the beginning . . .'

'What *we* have been saying from the beginning, Inspector. Never forget, we are a team. The efficiency of any policework is to be found in the measure of its teamwork.' He dropped the piece of ensaimada on to the plate, tore off another and proceeded to fiddle with that. 'What the devil could have persuaded him to make so ridiculous a statement?'

'Statement?'

'Just because the yellow press in Britain has been criticizing us with ever-increasing hysterical venom . . .' He drank some coffee. His voice became rich with self-pity. 'A man in his position should be able to rise above petty pride and to resist pressures for false claims, even when the pressure stems directly from the Minister. I mean, merely in order to silence criticism and appease the Minister, to hold a news conference last night after my telephone call and to issue a statement in which all I said on a conditional basis was presented as proven fact . . .'

'Is that what he did?'

'Haven't I just said so,' snapped Suau, for the moment speaking with his usual decisiveness.

'So when you told him this morning what had happened, he . . .'

'He had absolutely no right to speak to me like that. If anyone has put him in danger of appearing to be a fool, it is certainly not I.' He ate the ensaimada, each time biting savagely into the feather-light confection.

Ten minutes later, they entered Room 324. The bed was unmade, with the single top sheet thrown back; a book, opened face downwards, lay on the movable table; on the bedside cabinet were four more paperbacks, a digital clock, and a transistor radio; the silk dressing-gown was half on the settee, half on the floor; the cupboard door was open and hanging inside were a lightweight sports coat and grey flannels, two white shirts and underclothes were on the single shelf, and a pair of shoes and a leather suitcase were under this. In the bathroom were toothbrush and a tube of toothpaste, an electric razor, and a set of silver-backed brushes and comb.

'Nothing to suggest why he discharged himself in such a panic,' said Suau, at the conclusion of their search. 'So what possibilities do we now have to consider? One, that he received a threatening telephone call; two, that he had a visitor who told him something which alarmed him; three, that he had been planning to leave the moment he was physically capable of doing so and nothing specific happened . . . But the time of the morning seems to make that unlikely . . . Question whoever was on duty on the main switchboard and find out if he received or made any calls during the night. Ask the night nurses if he had any visitors. Find out if that woman of his, Carolina, was in touch with him. Check Cifre's movements—was he on duty at the military base or at home, did he know where the Mercedes was garaged, does he have a good knowledge of cars . . .'

Alvarez sighed.

The porter in the block of flats in the Paseo Marítimo was as disdainfully superior as ever. 'Naturally I have heard of the señor's death,' he said, in the tones of someone who knew everything.

'Where did he keep his Mercedes?'

'In the garage.'

'Which is where?'

'Two floors below.'

'Have you any idea where it was last night?'

'Here, where it has been since he was injured. He arrived by taxi in the early hours of the morning, went up to his flat, came back down to the garage, and drove off.'

'Who was on duty here?'

'The night porter.'

'Did he pass any comment on how the señor looked or acted?'

'It is not for us to make such comments.'

'But you'll make 'em, all the same.'

The porter said resentfully: 'I understand he was in an excitable state.'

'Did your mate gather why?'

'No.'

Alvarez took the lift up to the sixth floor. He went down the carpeted passage to the flat and pressed the bellpush. Carolina opened the door. 'You!'

He stepped inside and shut the door. She was dressed in a gaily coloured frock and her eyes were unreddened from weeping. 'Perhaps you have not heard that the señor is dead?'

'Of course I have.'

'You mourn in your own way?'

'What are you trying to get at? D'you think I'm not feeling rotten about it underneath?'

'Underneath, I expect your main concern is that you've lost your meal ticket.'

'You just won't understand,' she said furiously.

'Can't, not won't.'

She turned and went into the sitting-room and he followed her. The cocktail cabinet was open and a partly filled glass was on top of it. She saw the direction of his gaze. 'I needed something to help the shock.' She waited for him to speak, but when he didn't, she continued: 'And why the hell shouldn't I pour myself a drink if I need one?'

'For one reason, it all belongs to someone else now.'

'Yes, to me!' she exclaimed triumphantly.

He shook his head. 'I've checked with Madrid. His will leaves everything to his wife.'

'You're lying.'

'On the contrary.'

'But ... but he always promised me that if anything happened to him he'd leave everything he owned in Spain to me.'

'Obviously, he changed his mind.'

'He promised me.'

'Maybe he learned you were betraying him.'

'Christ! you talk like a priest.' Her voice rose. 'You're joking, aren't you? He's left me this flat?'

'Everything he owns goes to his wife.'

'It can't. She's an old cow.'

He shrugged his shoulders.

'God, if it's true, I hope he . . .' She cut the words short.

He could guess roughly what she'd been going to say. He was shocked to discover that anyone could display such cupidity in the face of death and was about to say so when a change in her expression checked his words. He wondered what twisted thoughts were going through her mind?

'Well, what d'you want here?' she asked aggressively.

He said quietly: 'Señor Leach came up to this flat early this morning, didn't he?'

'And?'

'Where were you?'

'Where d'you think? In bed.'

'On your own?'

'Yes, on my own, you dirty-minded old man.' She walked over to one of the chairs and sat.

'What kind of emotional state was he in?'

'Mad.'

'Why d'you say that?'

'Because he didn't ring and say he was coming, he just banged in here and woke me up, frightening me close to death. And when I tried to find out why in the hell he'd left the hospital in the middle of the night, all he could do was go on and on about Agapito.'

'What was he saying about him?'

'He was talking so wild I couldn't understand him any longer.'

'Why did he come here?'

'To get his passport.'

'Didn't you ask him where he was going?'

'Yes, I did. And he was too crazy to tell me.'

'Crazy or scared?'

'I don't know, and I don't bloody care.'

He left. Had he not done so, he might have been tempted to give her the hiding she so richly deserved.

CHAPTER 18

The gentle wind was from the south and it brought with it an added heat from Africa that took the temperature over the hundred mark and even the holidaymakers were driven into whatever shade they could find. On the military base, it felt as if the air might at any moment burst into flame.

The colonel was an officer of the old school, hard, arrogant, and contemptuous of civilian rule. But he wasn't a fool and therefore knew that he had to give at least the appearance of respecting democracy. 'I'll have inquiries made,' he said, in his curt voice.

'Thank you,' replied Alvarez, aware—and amused—that his appearance had made a very poor impression.

'You can wait here.' It might have been intended politely; it sounded far more like an order. The colonel left.

It was a much nicer room than the previous one Alvarez had been in and he assumed, judging from a glass-fronted cabinet which contained a number of silver trophies and from the furnishings, that this was an officers' recreational room. Against the near wall was a display desk and under the glass top was a large leather-bound book open near the middle; both pages were handwritten, some lines in ink, some in pencil, and the right-hand page was stained across the top corner. Because much of the handwriting was cramped and he didn't have his glasses with him—they were a badge of age which he was still reluctant to wear—he was unable to read much of it, but a few entries were in a bolder hand and these he could; clearly, this was the log of a cavalry unit in the Civil War and there was a description in terse, unimaginative terms of a cavalry charge at the battle of Boadilla. The final words were 'Position taken. Casualties seven dead, twelve wounded.' Seven men had died, he thought, and twelve had been wounded, to what effect? Had they done any more than provide a footnote to history, now forgotten and ignored by everyone but relatives and members of their regiment? And yet in many parts of the world men were still being pressed into battle and although they had been exhorted and praised in terms of patriotism, few, if any, of the survivors would learn in time that their country would eventually be quite content to let them be relegated to unread footnotes . . .

A captain came in. A very different kind of a man from the colonel, he was outgoing and friendly. He sat on the edge of the large table and referred to a sheet of paper on which he'd made some notes. 'You want to know about Cifre's movements last night. As you probably know, at the moment the conscripts do two days on duty and then have two off.' He smiled sardonically. 'They don't complain about so much time off, of course, but it doesn't make for good soldiers. The real trouble is, from our point of view, that they're not in the army long enough to make it worthwhile to train them to used advanced technology equipment and so they stay with the old square-bashing and menial jobs and get bored to the bone. Still, that's our problem, not yours . . . Cifre started his two days off at eight hundred hours yesterday morning.'

'Did he leave the base?'

'Immediately. You'll find they're all very punctual when it comes to leaving.'

'I don't suppose you've any idea where he went?'

'None whatsoever.' The captain crumpled up the sheet of paper and threw it at a wastepaper basket; it hit the edge, fell back. 'Wouldn't like to tell me what all this is about, would you?'

'Trying to find out if he was involved in something. If he was, it'll be a very serious charge, if he wasn't, his only fault is to have fallen for a bitch of a woman.'

'If that were a crime, a hell of a lot more of us would end up criminals.'

Mostia was in the hills behind Palma; it was a village of many short, steep roads with very sharp turnings and not even the Mallorquins could drive quickly in it. The carpenter's shop was on the ground floor of a house that overlooked the small square, one of the few pieces of land that was even roughly level. Throughout the day, the whine of a circular saw, the shrill scream of a band saw, or the tapping of a hammer, could be heard right round the square.

The elder Cifre was making a pair of shutters when Alvarez entered. He was a small man, middle-aged, with grey, balding hair, a sharp, darkly complexioned face, and a left hand which lacked two fingers as the result of separate accidents. Typically, both his circular and band saws were still without safety guards. He briefly looked up at Alvarez, then returned his attention to joining together the four lengths of wood, the two long ones being grooved, to make the frame of one of the pair.

'I'd like a word,' said Alvarez.

Cifre laid the frame flat, turned and brought out of a box a handful of pre-cut slats; he laid these down by the side of the frame. 'A word about what?'

'Your son, Agapito. Where is he?'

He shrugged his shoulders, picked up a pot of glue from a stand on which it had been kept warm. 'He's not here; that's all I know.'

'Where was he last night?'

'Does that matter?'

'It might do.'

He deftly glued several slats in place, tapping each one with a wooden mallet to bed it firmly.

His assistant, a young lad who'd just left school, came in from the road, looked with brief curiosity at Alvarez, then went over to the smallest of the three workbenches and began to sandpaper a square of wood, from time to time offering it up to a panelled door.

Cifre tapped home the last of the slats, picked up the shutter and set it upright against the nearby wall. 'Is he in trouble?'

'I don't know yet.'

He chose a broad chisel and felt the edge, reached over for a stone, worn by use, and carefully honed the blade. 'I wanted him to join me here. These days, people are spending money on their houses and there's work enough for the two of us. But he wouldn't.'

'Because of Carolina?'

He showed no surprise that Alvarez should have known about her. 'I said, and the wife said, she's a tart, just like her mother. But none of the young'll listen these days; think we're bloody old fools. But we've seen it all before; they haven't invented the world.' He tested the edge of the chisel again. 'Her mother went off with a man because he threw the pesetas around; she went off with some foreigner who lives in Palma. Good riddance, I told Agapito, but he wouldn't listen. Off day after day on that motorbike of his, his tongue hanging out for the tart.' He collected together the four pieces of wood which would form the frame of the next shutter.

'Has he seen her recently?'

'Ask him, not me. He don't speak much to me unless he's broke and needs money. The wife keeps giving it to him. Mothers are soft.'

'Mine isn't,' said the assistant, joining in the conversation.

'With you around, she can't afford to be.'

The assistant laughed loudly.

'Was he in the house yesterday evening?' Alvarez asked.

'Came back after we'd gone up to bed.'

'Did he stay in for the rest of the night?'

'As far as I know.' He began to join the four lengths of wood together.

'Would you have heard him go out again?'

'Not me; I don't hear that kind of noise so well now. But the wife would've.'

'When did he leave here this morning?'

'After getting up a couple of hours past when it should've been. I asked him to give a bit of a hand, seeing as a load of extra work's come in, but he said he'd too much to do.' He spoke without any change of tone; if he felt added resentment, he gave no indication of it.

A man entered from the square and said he wanted two metres of four by six and Cifre went over to a pile of odd lengths of wood and began to look through them. Alvarez called out his thanks, left. He skirted a pile of sand and another of small chippings, outside a house which was being reformed, and walked over to his car. If the Mercedes had been sabotaged, this could have been done any time after Leach had been admitted to hospital. Agapito Cifre's absence from home the previous evening, then, was not of itself of any significance. But if he were guilty of the murders, he would probably suffer the compulsion from which nearly all guilty people suffered, namely to deny anything which might even hint at his guilt without ever stopping to work out whether in fact it did. So he'd probably try for an alibi and claim he'd been at home. If he did this, here would be an indication—though not a strong one—of his guilt . . . If he were guilty, it was a reasonable assumption that he would make contact with Carolina as soon as possible to discover if there were any signs that he was suspected. He might even have been in the flat earlier on, listening to what had been said. Carolina would surely not be expecting a second visit from the police so soon after the first . . .

He drove from Mostia into Palma, finding the suburbs unusually free of traffic so that he made very quick time down to the Ronda and along to the Paseo Marítimo and the flat.

Carolina opened the door. 'Not you again!'

She'd shown no signs of panic, only of resentment. He stepped inside.

'Would you like to come in?' she asked with heavy sarcasm. She turned and went through to the sitting-room. 'All right, what's it this time?' she demanded, as she stood by one of the windows. The harsh sunlight formed a shaft of light behind her and this made it obvious that she was not wearing a petticoat under the flouncy dress. Disliking her as much as he did, he still stared.

'I said you were a dirty old man.'

He cursed himself for having given her that chance to jeer at him. 'When did you last see Agapito Cifre?'

'You've come back to ask that? You either need your head or your bloody ears examined. I told you, I finished with him years ago.' She turned towards the window; something on a finger caught the sunlight and flashed brief sparkles of fire. Then restlessly, she turned back, crossed to a chair, and sat.

'You haven't seen him in this past week?'

'That's right, I haven't.'

'You're certain?'

'D'you want me to swear to it on a stack of Bibles?'

'There wouldn't be much point to that, would there?'

She was about to shout abuse at him when she caught the expression in his eyes. 'Look, I've finished with him, right? So why should I see anything of him now?'

'Despite everything that's happened, he's still very fond of you.'

'That's up to him.'

'And because he's very fond of you, he was very jealous of Señor Leach. That gave you two strong emotions to play on.'

'What in the hell are you talking about?'

'To play on and so persuade him to murder Señor Leach so that you could inherit the señor's money.'

Her expression was shocked. 'You're not serious?' she

shouted. 'Why are you talking so bloody silly? You told me, everything's been left to his old cow of a wife.'

'Until I told you, you were convinced he'd left everything to you.'

'No, I wasn't. All I said was, I thought maybe . . .'

'You were convinced,' he said flatly. 'And therefore you reckoned that if he died, you'd inherit the lot.'

She began to cry. 'I didn't do anything,' she wailed. 'I swear I don't know anything about how he died.'

'Is Agapito here in the flat now?'

'Him . . . Here?'

He was certain her bewilderment could not have been simulated. 'When did you last see him?'

'I've told you, haven't I? When we split up. I wouldn't see him, not while I was with Cyril.'

'Living in Señor Leach's flat on his money didn't stop you entertaining the pilot last Saturday.'

'It's not the same. Agapito's a peasant . . .' She stopped, frightened by his expression.

'As I am a peasant,' he said harshly. 'And when everyone on this island was a peasant, it was a cleaner place.'

She sobbed. He watched her and for once another's distress evoked no sense of pity within him; she was not a victim of circumstances, but of her own ambitions and false values.

She said, in a shaky voice, deliberately sounding as distressed as she could: 'I need a drink. D'you want one?'

'No.'

She hesitated, as if wondering whether to defy the contempt behind his curt refusal. Then she stood and went over to the cocktail cabinet and poured herself a strong whisky. As she returned and passed him, he saw once again a quick sparkle of light from one of her fingers. She noticed his sudden interest in her hand and instinctively made the mistake of trying to hide it from him.

'Where did you get that ring?'

She reached her chair and sat. She shrugged her shoulders, said with studied casualness: 'I bought it months ago; it's only a bit of costume jewellery.'

'Let me see it.'

'Why?'

'I want to examine it.'

'It's none of your bloody business.'

'Give it to me.'

It was a clash of wills which she lost. She drank quickly, put the glass down, pulled the ring off her finger and held it out.

He knew very little about jewellery, but was certain that no one would ever bother to put a fake diamond in so exquisite a setting. Nor did he believe that any manmade stone could produce such colour-filled, ice-bright light. 'This isn't costume jewellery,' he said flatly, as if he could judge beyond any shadow of doubt. 'The diamond's genuine and valuable. Where did it come from?'

She picked up the glass and drank. 'He . . . he gave it to me.'

'When?'

'Just after I moved in with him.'

There was an unmistakable, if not easily defined, newness about the ring. He remembered how, on his previous visit, when he'd first told her that Leach's wife had inherited everything and she had inherited nothing, she'd been disbelieving and shocked and then how she'd suddenly looked as if she were exulting over something and he'd briefly wondered what twisted thought had just occurred to her. 'You bought this after I was here this morning,' he said with continuing certainty.

'No, I didn't.'

'When Señor Leach came here for his passport, he must have wanted money as well as cheque-books and credit cards; so somewhere in this flat there was a sum of money in cash. He didn't take very much because the law forbids the export of more than a certain amount and he was the kind of man who was scared of breaking the law. So he asked you to watch over it for him. And when you heard he was dead and his wife would inherit everything, you decided to steal what was left.'

'I swear that's not true.'

'This ring would have cost a great deal and there aren't many jewellers in Palma who have such expensive items in stock. It's easy enough to have every one of those questioned to find out if they've sold a ring to a woman of your description. If you're identified as having bought this ring, but you've continued to deny it right up to that identification, it'll be obvious that you know you had absolutely no right to that money and stole it.'

She began to cry again and this time her distress was not exaggerated. 'He owed it to me. He promised he'd always look after me. It wasn't stealing.'

'Where was the money?'

'In the safe in the bedroom,' she said in a low, strained voice.

The safe was behind one of the pictures and it had a combination lock. She gave him the combination. He had expected there to be little or no money left, but there were several bundles of dollar notes, all of large denominations.

CHAPTER 19

The sun was still hot even though it was early evening and shadows were creeping quickly across the land; the wind had died away, as it usually did at this time, and the air was completely still; to the north, the sky was becoming stained with mauve.

Alvarez left his car and walked towards Ca'n Orpoto. Zoe must have returned by now. He'd ring and she'd open the door and her face would light up with mischievous pleasure as she started teasing him; but they both knew that this teasing concealed the strongest of all emotions. And after a while, because they were mature enough to have learned that there was added pleasure to be found in waiting, she'd signal her surrender and together they'd move into a world where there was only happiness . . .

He rang the bell and waited for the sounds of her approach. There was silence. He rang again. She'd probably been out on the patio, drawing into her bronzed body the last of the sun, and had had to slip on something in case the caller was not he . . . He rang a third time.

He turned slowly away and walked back to the car.

Suau had expected the telephone call to be a difficult one, but he had not expected Superior Chief Salas's reaction to be so vehement. He tried to explain. 'He thinks he must speak to Señora Leach because . . .'

'He's suggested going to England and you've agreed that he should?'

'In the circumstances . . .'

'Every time that damned man has anything to do with circumstances, he turns them inside out. What did I tell you when I first said I was ordering him to work with you?'

'On no account allow him to complicate the issues. But . . .'

'So what happens? One evening you inform me we are dealing with a case of terrorism and the terrorists have escaped to Algeria . . .'

'Señor, it's not correct that I . . .'

'The next—the very next evening—you say that you agree with him that he ought to fly to England to make inquiries because he's found a large sum of money which will explain why Leach was murdered and the first two murders were not the act of terrorists. If that's not complicating and confusing issues, just tell me what bloody is?'

'I really don't think you should blame me because the evidence . . .'

'I blame you for letting him make a fool out of you. I blame you for categorically assuring me one day that it was an act of terrorism and the very next reversing your decision.'

'Señor, I must protest . . .'

'Do you begin to realize the position in which your incompetence has landed me? I have assured everyone that we are as capable and as efficient as any force in the world and in proof of this is the fact that it has taken us only seven days to prove that the murders were the work of terrorists and that they fled to Algiers; I have said that if the Algerian CID conduct themselves even half as efficiently as we, they will arrest the two terrorists within hours; I have pointed out that many other countries, even those who most pride themselves on the quality of their detective forces, have failed to identify terrorists who have carried out acts of terrorism in their lands; I have pledged the honour of my men, of my command, of the entire force, of the people, of the government, of Spain . . . And now you tell me that I may be forced to admit that I was wrong. And you have the stupidity to tell me you must protest!' He cut the connection.

Suau slammed his hand down on the desk. He'd make Alvarez rue the day he'd been born. He'd break his incompetent career into a thousand pieces and throw the pieces to the four winds . . . And then Suau began to think more coolly. If it proved not to have been an act of terrorism, Superior Chief Salas was going to be very angry; small-minded men when angry became vindictive. He would try to put all the blame on his comisario. But he wouldn't succeed if it could be shown beyond any shadow of doubt that his comisario's report had never stated flatly that the boat had been blown up by terrorists, but had always carried a strong qualification pointing out that there could be no certainty until all the facts were known . . . Alvarez could back him up. But Alvarez might be a little reluctant to do so if he'd been charged with incompetence, negligence, irresponsibility . . .

Suau slammed his hand down on the desk a second time.

Dolores served herself last of all and put two spoonfuls of fideos a la Catalana on her plate, hesitated, then added a third. The doctor had recently told her that she was several kilos overweight, but on hearing this Jaime had remarked that he didn't want to be married to a walking skeleton and there were times when she was prepared to listen to him.

'It's good,' said Alvarez.

She nodded.

'I liked it better last time,' said Juan, precociously trying to be funny. His mother looked at him and he belatedly realized that there were some subjects about which only a fool joked.

Jaime filled his tumbler with red wine and pushed the bottle across the table. Alvarez said, as he poured: 'I'm off to England tomorrow.'

A few years back, such an announcement would have been greeted with shocked surprise and apprehension, but since then his work had taken him abroad sufficiently often for the forthcoming journey to be accepted quite matter-of-factly by the family.

Juan stayed silent for as long as he could, then he said excitedly: 'I want some of those chocolate bars.'

'"I want" never gets,' snapped Dolores.

'But if I don't say what I want, how will Uncle Enrique know what to buy me?'

'He will have far too much to do to buy you anything.'

'No present?'

Isabel, who had already learned the value of an indirect approach, said: 'Verónica was given a doll by her English granny; it's the most lovely doll I've ever seen.'

'Her granny's rich,' said Dolores.

'I wish we were rich. Verónica's horrid and won't let anyone else play with her.'

'What's the doll look like?' asked Alvarez.

'She's this big.' She held her hands about thirty centimetres apart. 'And she's got long, curly hair, and freckles, and she says 'Mama', and when you press her tummy she wets herself.'

'And what's the little boy do when you press his tummy?' asked Jaime.

'Be quiet,' snapped Dolores.

'I do wish I'd a doll like her,' said Isabel wistfully.

'You've more toys as it is than you can play with.'

'But she's so lovely. And Verónica's such a beast and always boasting about her rich English granny.'

'D'you know what I'd ask for if I had a rich English granny?' asked Jaime.

'No,' said Dolores, 'and we don't want to, either.'

Alvarez cleared his throat. 'I've been wondering, Dolores, if you'd do something for me while I'm away?' He'd thought about this and had judged it best to ask her in front of the family so that she would feel constrained not to express her opinions too forcibly.

'What do you want?'

'Just to telephone someone and explain that I've had to fly over to England, but I'll be back very soon.'

'Who is it?' Her tone made it clear that she'd guessed the answer.

'Señora Williams.'

Her lips tightened. If he wanted a woman—and why shouldn't he?—why couldn't he forget the foreigners and find a Mallorquin widow with property? Foreign women were immoral, lazy, and spendthrifts, and one of them could only bring him unhappiness; a Mallorquin widow was moral, justly proud of the spotless cleanliness of her home, and when it came to money she had eyes of stone and hands of steel.

'Is that the señora who's after your soul?' asked Jaime, grinning lecherously.

Alvarez cursed the day he'd mentioned that.

Alvarez had previously discovered that although nothing would prevent his imagination picturing all three engines suffering flame-outs at the same moment, a wing cracking and ripping off, an explosive de-pressurization, a mid-air collision, and undercarriage failure on landing, a reasonable number of brandies did distance him from his fate. So the four brandies he'd had on the two-hour flight, which were in addition to the two he'd had in the departure lounge, enabled him to look out of the port and watch them coming in to land with no more than a brief prayer that his end might be painless.

Twenty-five minutes later, he collected his suitcase from the carousel, walked through the green channel and carried on into the main hall. A small crowd of friends and relations were waiting and he passed through them.

'Inspector Alvarez?'

He turned.

'Detective-Constable Irons; Theodoric Stephen, usually known as Steve.' He grinned, a lopsided grin which complemented his bent nose. 'I had a rich bachelor uncle who was called Theodoric and me being given the same Christian name was meant as a subtle compliment and hint. I never learned whether he felt complimented, but since he left all his money to charity, he obviously didn't take the hint. After that, I was damned if I was going to labour under such a disadvantage as Theodoric, so I switched to Steve!'

'Is that your only case?' He took the suitcase before Alvarez could object. 'D'you mind if we move smartly? I left the car on double lines. I explained the situation, but I don't know how generous the local lads are towards visitors from other forces. And if I turn up with another parking ticket, my guv'nor's going to blow his top.'

They reached a green Escort and to Irons's relief there was no ticket tucked behind the windscreen-wiper. He unlocked the doors and put the suitcase on the back seat. 'Is this your first time over here?' he asked, as he settled behind the wheel.

As they drove west along the motorway, Alvarez, while listening with part of his mind to Irons who was seldom silent, studied the countryside. Succeeding visits to England did nothing to lessen his surprise at the contrast between his own brown, parched, tight little island and this green, fertile land where it was commonplace to see a hundred head of sleek cattle in a single field. No wonder the British could flood into Mallorca, spending as if money really did grow on trees. His envy became coloured with bitterness. It was that money which had changed the lives of all the Mallorquins and almost destroyed their birthright. The past couldn't be changed. But that didn't stop one regretting it . . .

They drew up in the courtyard of a hotel on the outskirts of Steerford. 'I'll come on in with you and make certain everything's OK, then I'd better get back to the station; the guv'nor's one of those tiresome men who reckons an hour contains sixty-one minutes, if you know what I mean?'

'I do indeed. I have had to work with one such person recently.'

'A pain in the neck to everyone but their senior officers.'

And sometimes, thought Alvarez with pleasure, a pain in the neck to them as well.

They were shown to a room which overlooked the lawn that sloped down to the river. 'I sometimes take my kids out in a boat,' said Irons, as he looked out of the open window. 'A friend lets me borrow his . . . People I envy are the ones who do the real thing, like single-handed across the Atlantic. Are you a sailor?'

'No, I'm not.'

'Thought you might be, coming from a place like Majorca.'

'I suppose that really I am a farmer.'

Irons smiled. 'As far as I'm concerned, I'd rather buy my spuds and cabbages in the shops . . . OK, then, I'll be on my way. And see you tomorrow morning.'

'There is something before you go.'

'Sure. What is it?'

'I think it is necessary to find out if Señora Leach still lives at the address which I have and if she does, to arrange a meeting with her.'

'No sweat. Give me the address and I'll see to it. What kind of time d'you suggest? Something like eleven tomorrow morning?'

'That would be fine and there is just one more problem – I do not know if the señora is aware that her husband is dead.'

'Oh! . . . I hate having to break that sort of news, but it has to be done.' Irons said a final goodbye and left.

Alvarez went over to the window and stared out. An emotional man, he hoped that the señora would not be too shocked by the news of her husband's death if she had not heard about it before.

When Irons arrived the next morning, Alvarez was seated at one of the tables set out on the lawn. He called a waiter over. 'Coffee, please . . .' He turned to Irons. 'At home, it is the custom to have a brandy with the morning coffee. Would you like that?'

'I'll try anything once.'

The waiter, being English, showed his scorn for so degenerate a habit before he left to return into the building.

Alvarez pointed at the river. 'I've been sitting here for quite a time, just watching and enjoying. It's impossible in Mallorca to see a river flow because none do. And it's so soothing to watch water slide past like this; it makes the world seem so peaceful . . . Has someone spoken to the señora?'

'I have.' Irons brought a pack of cigarettes out of his pocket, offered it, then flicked open a lighter. 'And it's the damnedest thing! I'd braced myself for the usual emotional storm, but she showed virtually no emotion and said that it was the judgement of God.'

'Had she heard about his death before?'

'No.'

'And she showed no sorrow?'

'I don't think I've ever seen anyone less shocked by such news.'

'Of course, they had been separated for some time, but even so . . . If there was no emotional feeling left, I wonder he willed everything to her and failed to leave anything to Carolina. There surely has to be some explanation . . .' He was silent for a moment, then he said: 'Did the señora want to know how he'd died?'

'I told her at the beginning it had been a car crash, but she didn't ask for any details, like did he die instantly, as people usually want to know.'

'Perhaps the shock will come later, when she fully understands the meaning of what you've told her?'

'Somehow, I don't think it will.'

Could two people who'd once loved enough to marry really reach so sterile a relationship? wondered Alvarez sadly.

CHAPTER 20

Earls Avenue, on the far side of the town from the river, was a street of semi-detacheds which dated from the mid-'thirties. All the houses had been built to the same design and the monotony of repetition was only broken by differing colours, the occasional window extension, and in many cases the garages which had been erected in what had previously been front gardens—when the houses had been built, it had not been envisaged that the owners would ever be in a financial position to run cars. It was not a dismal road, since the houses were solid and largely well maintained, and some of the remaining gardens were bright with colour, yet something about it spoke of lives of dull, if worthy, inconsequence.

No. 14 needed repainting, it had no garage, and the front garden looked as if it hadn't been dug over that year. Irons rang the bell and the door was opened by Mrs Leach. She was a tall woman with a Grandma Moses face in which there was far more evidence of disapproval than compassion. She was dressed in a brown frock cut on severe, unflattering lines which accentuated her thinness.

"Morning, Mrs Leach.' Irons's manner was more subdued than usual. 'This is Inspector Alvarez from Majorca who I told you about.'

Alvarez said: 'Señora, I am very sorry to have brought such bad news.'

'I've been expecting it.'

Despite what Irons had earlier told him, her response shocked him; it almost seemed as if she were gaining some sort of satisfaction from her husband's death.

She opened the door more fully and they went in. The small, oblong hall was immaculately clean and tidy. The sitting-room was the same and this suggested it was never used, but there was a small black and white television set on a stand and that day's copy of the *Daily Mail* was lying, folded, on a table. The furniture was all large, far too large for the room, and well worn; the heavy three-piece suite was covered in an institutional brown cloth and no other colour could quite so readily have introduced a note of stern rectitude. She sat down in one of the armchairs and folded her hands in her lap.

'Señora, a moment ago you said that you had been expecting the sad news—why was that?'

'It was inevitable.'

'But perhaps you would explain why?'

'No, I will not.'

Alvarez looked at Irons, who shrugged his shoulders. Was she mentally unstable? wondered Alvarez. Yet he'd seldom met a woman who appeared to be more fully in control of herself. 'Señora, it would be very kind of you if you would answer one or two questions . . . Did you know that nine days ago Señor Leach went for a trip on a boat and while at sea there was an explosion which killed two and injured your husband and another man?'

She still failed to show any emotion. 'How could I know that?'

'He did not ring you from the hospital?'

'No.'

'When did you last speak to him?'

'I have not communicated with him from the day he left this house.'

'How long ago was that?'

'Six years.'

'Has he been in touch with you at all?'

'He has written letters.'

'But you did not answer them?'

'No.'

'Why not?'

'That is my business.'

'Perhaps, señora, it will help you to understand better why I'm here and asking these questions if I explain what happened. At first, we belived the boat had been blown up by terrorists who had meant to murder Señor Todd, one of the two who died. But then we became much less certain and decided that perhaps the motive had been entirely different and non-political and the intended victim had not necessarily been Señor Todd. During the course of the investigations I had to question your husband when he was in hospital to try and find out if anyone might have had a reason for wishing to kill him; after his death, I had to try to decide whether the crash had been an accident or an act of murder, following an unsuccessful attempt to murder him in the boat.

In these circumstances, it became necessary to examine his
life very carefully to discover whether or not there has ever
been cause for anyone to wish him dead and this can usually
best be done by asking questions of people who knew him
well. You may be able to help us determine whether he was
murdered and if he was, to identify the murderer.' He
paused, waiting for her to say something; she was silent.
'Would you tell me why he left home?'

'I will not.'

'Were there emotional problems?'

'I have just told you, I will not answer.'

'Do you not understand that I need to know if I'm to solve
the problem of his death?'

She pressed her thin lips even more tightly together and
shook her head.

'If he was murdered, you surely want the murderer
brought to justice?'

'I will not tell you.'

'Very well . . . Was he a rich man?'

In what was an eloquent, if silent, answer, she looked
round the room at the tired furniture and poor state of
decoration.

'But when he left here, he did have a reasonable amount of
money?'

'No,' she answered, very sharply.

'Are you sure?'

'Yes.'

'How was he able to afford to live abroad, then?'

'I've no idea.'

'Have you had financial problems, señora?'

'No.'

'Then you have an income of your own?'

Very reluctantly, she said: 'He sent money every month.'

'But if he did not have much money when he left here, and
he did not have a job in Mallorca, how could he afford to send
you money each month?'

'I do not know.'

'Was it always the same amount?'

'For a time.'

'And then?'

'He sent more. I have always given the extra to charity.'

And yet, thought Alvarez, it was obvious that she was having to keep within so tight a budget that any extra money would normally have been exceedingly welcome. 'Do you realize that when he died, he owned a luxurious flat?'

'I didn't, but I'm not surprised.'

'And he was in possession of a large sum in cash. Where do you imagine all this came from?'

'I keep telling you, I do not know.'

'The amount of money is so great that I must find out where it originated. Under his Spanish will, you are his sole beneficiary and therefore if we can be certain the money and the flat were legitimately his, they will become yours. You must see that it is very much in your interests to help me.'

'I know nothing.'

Irons said: 'Or you just won't tell us?'

She ignored the question.

'Did he leave here because he was in some sort of trouble?'

'No,' she replied vehemently.

'Who did your husband work for?'

'I don't remember.'

'I'm sorry, but I can't believe that. You do realize, do you, that I've only to initiate inquiries with the Department of Health and Social Security and the Inland Revenue to find out?' He paused, then said again: 'Who did he work for?'

She answered in a voice so low they could only just hear her: 'Sims Security.'

Irons looked across to see whether Alvarez wanted to ask any more questions, then stood. 'Thanks for your help, Mrs Leach. I'm sorry if we've distressed you. Please understand that we have to . . .'

'Why won't you go?'

They went.

Sims Security occupied two uglily functional buildings on the eastern outskirts of Stoneless, a small town six miles from Steerford. A notice just inside the main entrance to the grounds proudly proclaimed that two years previously the firm had been granted a Queen's Award for the design and manufacture of computer security systems. Reception was in the nearer building, a small office in which two secretaries worked in front of word processors. Irons asked to speak to the manager. They were shown into a well-carpeted room that contained an oval table around which were set several chairs and one large coloured photograph, framed, which had a small plaque underneath to say that this was the presentation of the Queen's Award.

A middle-aged man hurried in and shook hands. 'The name's John Tidmarsh,' he said, with the instant friendliness of a good PR man. 'So what brings the police to our neck of the woods?'

'Before I explain,' replied Irons, 'may I introduce Inspector Alvarez from Majorca?'

'Majorca, eh? We used to hold our sales conferences there, until the economic downturn. Very popular, especially the gin at something under a pound a litre.'

'Inspector Alvarez is investigating two, or maybe three, murders.'

Tidmarsh responded immediately to the solemnity of the subject. 'Sorry to hear that. It's becoming a hell of a world to live in; violence everywhere . . . Now, how can we possibly help in a murder case which, presumably, occurred in Majorca?'

'I need to know something about a man who once worked for you, señor,' said Alvarez.

'Someone from here has got himself mixed up in a murder case? I must say, that doesn't sound very likely!'

'Señor Cyril Leach.'

His perturbation was immediate and obvious.

Irons said: 'He left your firm roughly six years ago; why did he leave?'

Tidmarsh, his expression one of worried uncertainty, hesitated, then he said: 'I think perhaps you'd better have a word with Mr Ball. I won't be a minute.' He hurried out of the room.

'All the signs are,' murmured Irons, 'we've opened up a can of worms.'

Ball was small, very precise in manner, and he made no attempt to be other than hostilely businesslike; he did not offer to shake hands. 'I understand you're making inquiries about Leach. I think it will be best if I make it clear right from the beginning that it is not our policy to discuss our staff, whether or not they are still with us.'

'Not even when it's a police matter?'

'I can conceive no way in which Leach's work here can have the slightest bearing on a murder case in Majorca.'

'Inspector Alvarez has already said that it may have.'

'Señor,' said Alvarez, 'what work did he do here?'

Ball considered the question for some time before replying. 'We're a small firm and the only way we can compete in the market place is to be more efficient or more innovative than the larger firms or to target an area in which it doesn't pay them to compete; because of this, all the technical staff are expected to have the skills to work in all departments. It is impossible to categorize Leach's position beyond saying that he was not normally employed in a task where initiative was at a premium.'

'Categorize it inexactly,' said Irons.

Ball looked at him with dislike. 'He was not good at initial design, but he did have the ability to turn someone else's design into a practical working unit.'

'Presumably we're talking about computers?'

'Safe computer circuits.'

'That means, ones that can't be hacked?'

'In this sense, it's probably wrong to use the word "can't". I would prefer to say, ones which it is very, very much more difficult to enter without the proper authorization.'

'You're like a specialist locksmith, advising and helping other people not to be burgled?'

'If you wish to use such an analogy.'

'Why did he pack up working here?'

'He resigned.'

'For what reason?'

'When a man says he wishes to leave, it's the firm's policy to accept his request without inquiring into the reasons. We have no wish to employ someone who will no longer be offering one hundred per cent of his effort and loyalty.'

Irons waited, then said: 'That seems to be everything, then. Thanks for your help.'

Ball nodded.

Irons took the two glasses of beer from the barman and carried them across to a table just beyond the dartboard. He handed one to Alvarez, sat. 'I'll tell you one thing. If I was in trouble and needed a shoulder to cry on, I wouldn't waste my time seeing if Ball's was free. He's one very cold fish.'

'In Spain, we would say . . .' He stopped, smiled briefly. 'We would say, he acts like an Englishman.'

'Stiff upper lip and all that? . . . Well, here's mud in your eye.' He drank. 'What do you think of our real ale, brewed not far up the road?'

'It is very pleasant,' replied Alvarez diplomatically. He would have far preferred a brandy, but had not been willing to put Irons to such an expense. 'Tell me something. What can we do now about finding out what happened when Señor Leach left the firm?'

'I've been giving that a bit of thought.' Irons wiped his mouth with the back of his hand. 'D'you remember how reluctant Mrs Leach was to give us the name of the firm? And how hail-fellow-well-met Tidmarsh was until we mentioned Leach's name, whereupon he clammed up tighter than an oyster and very hurriedly handed over to Ball? To my mind, that all adds up to a different story from the one Ball gave us, that Leach merely resigned. The problem then becomes, if neither she nor the firm will tell us the truth, who the hell will? . . . And that's got me remembering a chap I've done some sailing with who I know works for Sims. If I tackle him on a pal-to-pal basis, he may be able to tell me something. As we say, there's more than one way of killing a cat.'

'With us, there's more than one vegetable one can grow in the ground.'

'Comes to the same thing. Except for the cat, of course.'

Irons arrived at the hotel at six-fifteen that evening; Alvarez was again outside, watching the river and the several pleasure boats on it.

'Eureka!' said Irons, as he sat.

'You have discovered what happened?'

'I have. And as the explorer said when he came home fifteen months after setting out to find his wife nursing a newborn baby, how very unexpected. Leach was clearly a man of more initiative than his bosses ever realized. He devised a system to beat the company's own computer and used it to defraud the company. Being consulting experts in security, they were exceedingly reluctant to prosecute when they discovered what had been happening, so they swallowed their pride and anger and got rid of him, but didn't call in the police.'

'How much did he steal?'

'My friend doesn't know the details.'

'The flat and the cash in the safe, added to the money Leach must have spent over the past six years, come to at least half a million pounds. Would that firm, which surely cannot have great resources, be able to suffer such a loss?'

'Certainly not without a hell of a lot of trauma since, even if they had some form of insurance which covered the loss, almost certainly they wouldn't be able to call on that if they didn't report the swindle to the police.'

'So we may perhaps not yet know all the story?'

'I reckon you're dead right, which is why we'll call on Ball again tomorrow . . . And now let's forget work. My missus has invited you to supper. Nothing grand, but she thought you might enjoy an English family meal?'

'It would be a very great pleasure.'

'If I were you, I'd wait to say that until you've eaten!'

Ball held his head, bald and shiny, aggresively thrust forward. He was wearing a dark charcoal pinstripe suit and the way in which the jacket hugged his thick neck and slight, sloping shoulders showed that it had been made by a first-class tailor. 'I had hoped that I'd made it quite clear I could tell you nothing more.'

'That's right,' agreed Irons cheerfully. 'But I reckoned that perhaps our sudden questioning had caught you on the hop, as it were, and later on you might have remembered a few more details which you'd want to pass on.'

'Then your reckoning was incorrect.'

'There wasn't, then, any question of fraud?'

Ball's expression tightened.

'It's not true that Leach had found a way of persuading the firm's computer to cough up credit to some bogus account which he could milk later on?'

Ball suddenly looked tired. 'All right,' he said bitterly, 'that's what happened.'

'And you let him get away with it?'

'What else could we do?'

'Prosecute.'

'And admit to the world that we, a company which advises other companies on how to avoid being defrauded, had been defrauded by one of our own employees? We'd have become a laughing-stock among the people who matter and we'd have been finished. Leach knew that as well as we did, which is the only reason why he dared set up the fraud in the first place.'

'Señor,' said Alvarez, 'did not the loss of half a million pounds, or more, nearly ruin you?'

'What are you talking about?'

'How much did he steal?' asked Irons.

'Thirty-five thousand four hundred and twenty-two pounds.'

'Is that figure quite certain?'

'D'you think I can't remember it down to the last penny?'

'But could he have taken a lot more which you don't yet know about?'

'Six years on? Impossible. In any case, at the time the accountants carried out an exhaustive investigation to determine the full extent of our losses.' Ball ran the palm of his right hand over the dome of his head. When he next spoke, it was the first time there had been any suggestion of friendliness in his voice. 'Do you know something really odd? If before it all happened you'd asked me who was the last man to do such a thing, I'd have named Leach. He was such a negative kind of a person.'

But not quite so negative as everyone had believed, thought Alvarez.

CHAPTER 21

Irons braked to a halt in front of No. 14, Earls Avenue, and switched off the engine. Alvarez said: 'When Leach first lived in Mallorca, he wasn't well off. But roughly three years ago, he was able to buy a luxury flat and a big car and live a very easy life. But there's been no indication of where the big money came from.'

'No lead in Majorca?'

'No. I came here hoping to find a fresh one.'

'Instead of which, all you've uncovered are more questions . . . Then we'll just have to pressure Mrs Leach into being more forthcoming than last time.'

They left the car, crossed the pavement, and went up the flagstone path with weeds growing between the stones, to the front door with its peeling paint. The rundown state of the property raised yet one more question, thought Alvarez. From the moment he'd left home, Mrs Leach had accepted money from her husband even though she had known he had stolen it. So why, when he'd given her more and she could have improved her life, had she refused the extra? Surely not on the grounds of morality? So was it, remembering her character, because in the first instance she had had to have the money to live, but in the second she did not so that she had been able to afford the luxury of abnegation?

She opened the door. She was wearing a fresh dress, but although it was newly laundered it was shabby from wear. Without a word, she let them in. Without a word, she led the way into the sitting-room where she immediately sat.

Irons, more sensitive to the additional distress he was about to cause her than his normal slap-happy attitude to life might have suggested, spoke quietly. 'Mrs Leach, yesterday we spoke to the managing director of Sims Security. He told us the circumstances in which your husband left the firm.'

Her cheeks reddened.

'He defrauded them of just over thirty-five thousand pounds, but they didn't call in the police because they wanted to hush up the theft. Did you know from the beginning what had happened?'

She spoke in a dead voice. 'He told me nothing until they found out. Then he wanted me to go to Majorca with him. I told him I could never do such a thing; he had broken the eighth commandment.'

'What did he say to that?'

'That the only commandment which mattered these days was the eleventh.'

'Eleventh?'

'He was blaspheming.'

'I realize that, but what did he mean by it?'

'I cannot repeat blasphemy.'

He changed the subject. 'Have you any idea how much money he had when he left this country?'

'All that he had stolen.'

'Had he defrauded anyone other than Sims?'

'He told me only about that theft.'

'You said he'd written to you more than once from Majorca. In any of his letters, did he ever mention finding a new source of money?'

'No.'

'Your husband left here with approximately thirty-five thousand pounds but, as far as we know, no more than that. For three years, or so, he lived quietly in Majorca. Then he became rich and bought a luxury flat and a big car and sent you more money. When he died there were three hundred thousand dollars in his safe. Can you suggest where all that might have come from?'

'From the Devil,' she said, and meant it literally.

Through the port, Alvarez looked down at the Pyrenees, the highest peaks of which were still touched with snow. He finished the brandy and, to prevent his fears surfacing too freely, asked a passing air stewardess to bring him another.

Where had that unexplained money come from? The obvious answer was, another swindle. But Leach had not had a job in Mallorca and there were no signs that he had carried out another, and very much larger, one in Britain . . . A man who had wanted to show the world he was not as negative as the world believed? . . . A man who had turned to crime because he had not the courage to abandon his wife, but had known that if she learned he was a criminal she would abandon him? . . . Would Todd ever have invited him aboard the *Aphrodite* had he known that he was a swindler? But then, of course, in a different sense Todd was as much a swindler, swindling husbands out of the love of their wives . . . And come to that, Kendall had also been a swindler, his victims the people who bought homes from him . . .

Sweet Mary! he said aloud, to the obvious consternation of the English spinster in the aisle seat. From early on in the inquiry, he had had the feeling that he was missing something important. Now he realized that that something was the answer to a question he should have asked himself at the beginning. Why had Todd, not a man ever to put himself out when there was nothing to be gained by doing so, have asked Leach and Kendall out for the day on his boat when apparently he'd nothing whatsoever in common with either of them? Once the question was asked, it became obvious that the word 'apparently' was all-important. Despite appearances, the three of them must have had something in common . . . They had. All three were swindlers.

Surely, in the light of this it was feasible to suppose that there had been a common motive for their murders, rather than that there had been a motive peculiar to one of them and the others had been killed or injured simply because they'd had the bad luck to be aboard the boat?

Each of the three had shown evidence of newly acquired wealth in the period three to four years previously; each of them was a swindler. Wasn't it obvious that they had carried out a swindle that had netted each of them a fortune? And that it had been a victim of this swindle who had murdered them . . .

The air hostess brought him another brandy. As he drank, he noticed that the Englishwoman in the aisle seat kept glancing at him, a look of apprehension on her face. Hadn't she ever seen a man drink before?

*

He gave Isabel a doll which spoke and wet her pants, Juan two sets of unused British stamps and four Mars Bars, Jaime a bottle of Glenfiddich malt, and Dolores a cashmere sweater. Dolores kissed him, her gratitude as much for his safe return as for the gift, and Jaime poured out two very large brandies. Alvarez settled down in his usual chair. It was good to be back in civilization.

Supper was a special meal. There were prawns—two thousand five hundred pesetas a kilo, Dolores told them twice, lest any of them should be in any doubt about the extent of the luxury they were enjoying—grilled with a garlic, parsley, and olive oil sauce, followed by chicken and rice mixed with sweet peppers, garlic, and mushrooms, beans with serrano ham, and finally bananas with almonds baked in their skins.

'We must have a little drink to celebrate,' said Jaime. He turned and reached across for the bottle of brandy. 'It's not every day that Enrique returns from abroad.'

'But it is every day that you manage to find reason to celebrate,' Dolores said tartly.

He poured brandy into the glass he'd used for wine, passed the bottle to Alvarez.

She stood. 'The table isn't going to clear itself. Isabel . . .'

'Please, I want to play with my doll.'

Juan, seeing his mother's gaze come round to him, hurriedly said: 'And I want to stick the stamps in my album.'

She sighed. She knew she was far too lenient—not only as a mother, but also as a wife—but there were times when it pleased the soul to be lenient. She began to stack up the plates, noticed that Alvarez obviously intended to help her. 'No, no, Enrique, you sit back and be lazy with the rest of them.'

'I couldn't possibly watch you do all the work.'

She was about to remark that usually he found absolutely no difficulty in doing just that, but checked the words, determined not to spoil his homecoming. She carried the plates out into the kitchen and put them down by the sink. Alvarez followed her. 'Dolores . . .' He stopped.

'Well?'

'I hope the sweater fits?'

'It's just as if it had been made for me.'

He hesitated, saw she was looking curiously at him, and hurried out.

She turned on the hot water tap. From outside, came the roar of the geyser as the main jet lit.

Alvarez returned with three tumblers. 'Has everything been all right while I've been away?' he asked as he put the tumblers down.

'Why shouldn't it have been?'

'Just wondered . . . So everything's gone along smoothly?'

'Except for Magdalena. She came here yesterday morning and said María had said that I had said Rosa was . . . You're not listening!'

He started. 'Of course I am.'

Her expression sharpened. The look now on his face explained why he'd offered to clear the table and why he was now standing around. She squeezed the plastic bottle of washing-up liquid with unnecessary force and the jet went too high and hit the tiles above the sink. The waste annoyed her even more.

He coughed and tried to speak very casually. 'I don't suppose you remembered to make that telephone call for me?'

'If you ask me to do something, I do it.'

'Oh!' It was as much a question as a meaningless exclamation. He waited, but she pushed past him, picked up the glasses from the table, returned to the sink and began to wash them. 'Did you speak to the señora?'

'No.'

'Because she was still away?'

'That's right.'

'Then perhaps you had a word with the maid?'

'Yes.'

'Did she say anything?'

'Only that the señora was not there and she'd no idea when she'd be back.'

'Oh!' he said for the second time. 'Well, thanks a lot for ringing.'

She wanted to say, Enrique, why won't you understand that life can never be how you try to see it? But she remained silent. His first evening home was no time to lecture him. Yet why was he so blind? It made her want to hit him for being such a fool at the same time as she comforted him for being so blind.

He walked up to the front door of Ca'n Orpoto, promising himself that she had returned and would greet him with all the eagerness he had for so long imagined. But she hadn't. And since it was a Sunday, neither was the maid there. He returned to his car. Someone had once said that it was better to travel hopefully than to arrive; some travels, however hopefully undertaken, were too painful to be prolonged.

He drove down to the harbour, walked along to the western end. Three fishermen were either mending nets or cleaning up, but none of them was Carbonell. He began to walk away, stopped, returned to the man who was mending a net and asked him how the fishing had been recently. The reply, given in surly tones, was that it had been terrible. Alvarez told a story about the tax collector who remarked that according to the fishermen and farmers on the island there had been continuous gales for the past five years. The man relaxed, recognizing a kindred spirit, and before long was talking freely. After a while, Alvarez asked him where the best fishing was to be found at the moment and he replied as a second man came up to them, having left his boat. 'South,' he said.

'What's south?' asked the newcomer, a much younger man.

'The best fishing. At this time of the year, it's always south.'

'Except when there's a westerly wind . . .'

'Always south,' he interrupted.

On the day of the explosion, Carbonell—recognized as an expert fisherman—had sailed to the east and had later reported a poor catch. Yet the harbourmaster had said that catches were very good. 'I was told a fortnight ago that the best fishing was to the east, even as far along as Cala Murada.'

'Who said that?' asked the elder fishermen contemptuously.

'A local.'

'Sounds like a local waiter.'

Alvarez chatted for a few more minutes, then left. He made his way through the drifting crowds of tourists and went up one of the back roads to the bar where he'd drunk with Carbonell on the Friday after the boat had blown up. A number of men were present, some playing the local card game to the normal accompaniment of heated arguments so that it sounded to anyone who didn't know the character of the game as if a fight were both inevitable and imminent. It was a couple of minutes before the owner of the bar came along and took his order for a coffee and a brandy. As he was served, he said: 'D'you remember me?'

'Can't say I do.'

'I was in a fortnight or so ago. I had the job of collecting the bits and pieces of the *Aphrodite*.'

The owner suddenly nodded. 'I remember now. You're something to do with the police. And you was in here with Vicente.'

'Right again. You've a memory like a computer.'

The owner was plainly gratified by the compliment. 'I've a mind for faces, always have had; as the wife says, I never forget one.' He conveniently forgot that only a very short time before he had initially failed to recognize Alvarez.

'I'm looking for Vicente now. No idea where I can find him, I suppose?'

'Have you tried down by the boats?'

'He's not there.'

'What about his house?'

'I'll go along when I leave here.'

'Still working on the case?'

'That's right.'

'I thought it was all over and done with. According to what I read, it was terrorists blowing up an English MP . . . Pity they can't do the same to some we've got.'

'That's all right by me, just so long as I don't get involved.' He drank the brandy. 'I could do with another. And how about you this time?'

He refilled Alvarez's glass and poured a drink for himself.

Alvarez said chattily: 'I've never forgotten the last time I was here you telling me about some of the coincidences you've met.'

'Is that right? . . . It's fact. I've come across more than a few in my time.

'There was the friend of your wife who lost her wedding ring and then found it when she dropped something else days later.'

'That's as true as I'm standing here.'

'And then there was your brother-in-law who was having tapas at a bar in Palma.'

'And got talking casual-like, as one does, to the man standing next to him and found out they'd been to school together!'

'Incredible, isn't it? And you also mentioned how strange it was that it should have been Vicente who picked up the two survivors from the boat . . . But for the life of me, I can't remember why that was a coincidence.'

There was a call from the other end of the bar and the owner hurried along and served a couple of men. That done, he returned and rested his elbows on the scarred and stained wood. 'You was wondering why it was a coincidence that Vicente picked 'em up. That's easily told. Some years back now, Félix Rullán was working in the boats—his dad had died and he'd given up the charcoal-making. All the boats were out one day when a wind suddenly came out of the clear sky, like it can at certain times of the year, and in next to no time the sea was as rough as hell. Vicente and his mate had an old boat then and the engine packed in and they couldn't keep the bows head on, so the next thing they knew, they was broached and sunk. Neither of 'em was much of a swimmer and anyways the sea was too rough for swimming and so they was close to drowning when Félix Rullán rescued 'em. This time, it was Vicente rescuing Félix. Like I've always said, the world's made up of coincidences!'

'That's right,' agreed Alvarez. Only this had not been a coincidence.

CHAPTER 22

As Alvarez stepped out of his car, he remembered himself saying to Rullán words to the effect that up here one lived in beauty and honesty, far above the ugliness and dishonesty below. He should not have forgotten that while no man was an island, no island was free of man.

The small dog, curly tail waving furiously, bounded up towards him, yapping excitedly; the chickens which had been briefly disturbed returned to their endless scratching; a pigeon floated down on to the roof of the house and sat on a ridge tile, preening; a nightingale, careless of the time of day, began to sing.

Rullán came up to the car. Alvarez said: 'I need to ask you a few more questions.'

Rullán, as expressionless as ever, led the way round to the patio; Alvarez continued on past him towards the edge of the land, careful as always not to approach so closely that he became affected. He stared down at the floor of the valley and at all the building which was in progress.

Rullán left the patio and joined him. 'It's not gone away,' he said sardonically.

'Cut a tree and you can plant another; plough a field and you can reseed it; build a house of stone and eventually the stones return to the land; but that destruction is forever. That's the real crime which has been committed . . . What was the name of the woman who once owned the whole valley?'

'Mad Magdalena.'

'Was she truly mad?'

'Who's mad, who's sane? She owned the valley but she dressed like a gipsy; she talked to herself more than she did to other people; she believed the pair of golden eagles were her brothers.'

'But you didn't think her mad?'

'Didn't matter what time of the day I went down, there was always grub for me; all the things I liked most but couldn't have at home because making charcoal never brought in much money. And she'd play for as long as I wanted to; we'd build castles, hunt for hidden gold, chase robber bands.'

'If she was like that when you were young, why didn't you warn her about the men who wanted her valley?'

Rullán spoke bitterly. 'When a boy grows up, he's often a bloody fool and thinks it's soft to go on doing the things he used to . . . I tried to explain to her that since I'd become a man I felt daft pretending to be looking for gold or capturing bandits. When she couldn't understand, she became excited, like always, and—God forgive me—I also started to think her mad. But you've got to believe me, I never stopped loving her even if I was married and wasn't seeing her.'

'And then the eagles were poisoned?'

'That was after she'd left the valley and moved into a place where the nuns looked after her. When they told her the eagles had died, it was her two brothers dying all over again, and that broke her heart. And so she died.'

'And with the eagles gone, there wasn't the same pressure from conservationists to preserve the valley?'

'They hadn't got the emotional power behind 'em they'd had before, so people weren't as ready to listen and be sympathetic. And on top of that, a lot of money was going into the pockets of people who were in a position to alter things. If you've the money, you can bribe any man but a dead one.'

'Was it money took your wife?'

'I don't know; I still don't bloody know.' As if attracted by the pain in his voice and wanting to offer comfort, the dog came up and nuzzled his leg. He bent down for a few seconds and stroked her head. 'Until they started down there, everything was all right. She wanted kids, but didn't seem to be able to have any; still, she was happy. We used to . . .' He stopped, rammed his hands into his pockets. 'When they began building, she got restless. Kept wanting me to take her down to see exactly what it was like; kept talking about the exciting life there'd be when everything was finished and how she'd be able to start really living. But I wouldn't take her. I couldn't go down there and watch 'em close to, destroying the valley I'd known. She wouldn't understand; said all I wanted to do was bury her alive . . . I came back one day and she was gone. Never seen her since. Though I've heard it's not been like she hoped.'

'So the men who bought this valley through trickery destroyed three people or things you loved; Mad Magdalena, your wife, and the valley. You had cause to hate them.'

'I'd cause enough, and more.'

'When did you decide to murder them?'

Rullán showed neither surprise nor fear at the question. He answered in the same level voice. 'One day, the señor left some papers on the boat. I saw one was about the valley, so I read 'em all. That's when I learned the three of 'em was the company what had bought the land.'

'Was the boat trip the first chance you had to kill them after that?'

'That's right. The señor usually never had anything to do with the other two.'

'Have you any idea why he invited them that Tuesday?'

'Because they were thinking of starting another development.'

'How d'you know that?'

'Heard a bit of talk when I was serving the meal; they'd drunk until they weren't bothering as much as usual what their tongues were saying.'

'Where were they going to destroy this time?'

'Didn't hear where. Doesn't matter now, does it?'

'Provided no one else gets the same idea . . . Why d'you use so much explosive? Didn't you care if you blew yourself up along with them?'

'D'you think I'm bloody daft? I reckoned to get 'em at the table and not sink the boat; I didn't know the quarry was using stronger stuff than they used to.'

'When you were in the water, didn't you hear Señor Leach calling for help?'

'He was shrieking like a woman.'

'Why didn't you swim over and help him?'

'Save that yellow bastard?'

'All right, then, why didn't you go across and shut him up by pushing his head under? Carbonell was half an hour away and couldn't see you.'

'Letting him drown was one thing; drowning him another.'

'But you'd just tried to kill him in the explosion.'

'And he'd escaped. It was the hand of God.'

'If you wouldn't try to kill him a second time, you didn't sabotage his car so that he crashed?'

'No.'

Leach, panicked by fear of retribution at the hands of Cifre, had driven too fast when physically not fit to drive at all. As a consequence, he had crashed. The hand of God had saved; the hand of God had destroyed.

After a long pause, Rullán said: 'What happens now?'

'I have to report to my superior, Comisario Suau.'

'He'll arrest me?'

Alvarez stared out at the scene which was beautiful until one learned the reality. If a man was accused of a crime, the law demanded he be tried and, if found guilty, punished; yet no one had learned how to make the law morally just.

Alvarez entered the building and went up to the third floor and Suau's office.

Suau said, with childish sarcasm: 'Do I congratulate you on reporting so promptly after your return? After all, it is only yesterday afternoon that you arrived.'

'I uncovered certain facts in England, señor, and because of these I considered it was best if I followed them through before reporting to you.'

'Best for whom?'

'I don't understand.'

'Best for you, or best for the successful conclusion of this case?'

'Señor, I have been able to identify—'

The telephone interrupted him. Suau answered the call and his manner became obsequious. 'Yes, señor . . . Of course, I do understand that, but . . . I hope you will see my position . . . No, señor . . . Yes, señor . . .' He replaced the receiver. 'Do you know who that was?'

'I imagine it was Superior Chief Salas.'

'You imagine! Why the hell has no one ever strangled your imagination? The laboratory reports that there are no signs that the Mercedes was sabotaged. In their opinion, the crash was an accident, brought about by loss of driver control. Which means that Leach was not murdered. And if no one

murdered him, all your imaginative theories are hogwash; so
much goddamn hogwash!'

If only they were, Alvarez thought sadly.

Outside the garage of Ca'n Orpoto there was now a car.
She was back. Excitement, anticipation, tension, washed
through him. She'd promise him with eyes which changed
shade and her body would speak to him and the gates of
paradise would be opened to them both . . .

She was dressed in a frock, far more conservative than
anything he had seen her wear before, and yet this very
conservatism highlighted her electric animalism.

'My favourite detective!' She linked her arm with his.
'What fun to see you again. Come on through.' As she drew
him inside, he felt the curves of her body briefly touch his
side. His mouth was dry, his pulse wild.

Out on the patio, two chairs were set near the table and
one was in the sun, the other in the shade; a man sat in the
shaded chair. In his early thirties, he was handsomely
rugged and almost as bronzed as she.

'Tim, this is my favourite Mallorquin detective.'

Tim waved a hand in greeting, but did not bother to stand.

'I want you to know that he's the sweetest man I've ever
met and the only one who's ever turned me down flat.'

'Impossible!' he said, with a coarse laugh.

'It's true.' She had released Alvarez's arm to go through
the doorway from the sitting-room out on to the patio; now,
she took hold of his hand. 'I positively threw myself at you,
didn't I, Enrique, but you behaved like a verray parfit gentil
knight and left my chastity untouched. Just tell the doubting
Thomas over there that that's the absolute truth.'

'Señora, I . . .' He stopped.

'Oh dear, I've embarrassed the man again and so
he's forgotten that my name is Zoe. Only nice people get
embarrassed, don't they, Tim?'

'Would I know?'

She released Alvarez's hand. 'It's one large brandy, lots of ice, no soda, neither shaken nor stirred, isn't it?'

'Señora, it is very kind of you, but I cannot stay. I only came to tell you that now we know who planted the bomb.'

'Hey, what bomb's that?' asked Tim.

'The one which blew up Deiniol,' replied Zoe.

'But that's history. Tell me something new.'

'Susan's moved in with Bill.'

'You've just got to be joking.'

'I promise you I'm not.'

'But Bill's shacked up with Pam.'

'Not since the end of last week.'

'The randy old goat,' he said enviously.

Their real interests lay only in their own little world. Alvarez turned away.

'You really do have to go, Enrique? What a pity! But you must promise to come and see me again some time . . . You can find your own way out, can't you?'

Alvarez went through the house to the hall. He stopped and looked at the picture of the leopard and he was certain that now it was sneering. He opened the front door and went out, turned back to close the door and caught sight of his reflection in the newly affixed mirror on the opposite wall. And he saw not the image which he had been imagining, that of vibrant, irresistible maturity, but the image she had seen, presumptuous middle age, so amusing to tease for just so long as there was no one young and virile on call . . .